# THE ORVIS ANTHOLOGY

The C. F. Orvis Outdoor Writing Awards

*Edited by Tom Rosenbauer*

*Foreword by John Merwin*

*Illustrations by Ernest Lussier*

RIVERWOOD PRESS

Library of Congress Cataloging in Publication Data

Main entry under title:
The Orvis anthology.

    1. Hunting—Addresses, essays, lectures.  2. Fishing—
Addresses, essays, lectures.  3. Game and game-birds—
Addresses, essays, lectures.  I. Rosenbauer, Tom.
SK33.0736    1984     799     84–4713
ISBN 0–8289–0527–4

# Contents

# Foreword

WHEN I FIRST STARTED publishing my own magazine, I looked hard for ways to attract attention in an overcrowded arena. I then realized that within all that's encompassed by our arts and letters there have been few areas less subject to—and more deserving of—criticism than what's commonly called outdoor writing. After some discussion, the very first issue carried a scathing commentary on our hook-and-bullet press, written by the late Bob Deindorfer. The writing community was stirred considerably, both pro and con. Readers, never having seen a fishing publication examine its own field so critically, were for the most part delighted. For what it was worth, we got the attention we sought.

Unfortunately, the ripples of that moment have long since died. We influenced, perhaps, a few fledglings, but we didn't make any good writers better, nor did we improve the outlook of those who persist—year after year—in cranking out stories that are just plain bad writing. I have been sufficiently frustrated by all of this to have produced, on a few occasions, some near-venomous criticism. This has delighted a few people, mostly because they agreed with me, but also because that sort of thing finds its way to a printed page so seldom. One of the Canadians involved in this book's publication asked a few months ago if (chuckle, chuckle) I couldn't incorporate some of that into a foreword.

Well, I will. It is hard, after all, to resist shooting when the birds are flying so slowly. But I will try, too, to be a little more constructive than in past writing. It should, I think, be our mutual object to improve the state of things, which will require both a shotgun and a box of Band-Aids.

It was to my considerable amusement that the same friend who solicited me for this foreword also solicited my comments on a story he'd written for a national fly-fishing publication. He had taken a tour of southern British Columbia, fishing steelhead rivers about which Roderick Haig-Brown had earlier and most gracefully written. The story consisted of my friend's modern observations interspersed with long Haig-Brown quotes describing the same water. Not a bad idea, if one writes as well as the late Haig-Brown. My friend does not, although he writes adequately.

The telephone explanation went something like this: Do your own story, Charlie. And don't make yoursef look bad.

"What do you mean? How'd I make myself look bad?"

"Charlie! Haig-Brown was an excellent writer. You're not. Suppose you were an attractive woman who wished to be noticed at a dinner party. (Don't shoot, madam, I'm not stereotyping.) Given a choice, you certainly wouldn't sit next to Miss Universe, but that's just what you did in your story."

His dreams, he confessed, were a little shattered, but constructively so. He is finding, as some people who write never do, that writing itself is a craft. As such, it requires both study and practice. And as such, it deserves some respect from its practitioners that isn't always accorded.

It's regrettable that much of the tradition behind our writing about hunting and fishing is pegged on a simple information transfer. Which rifle to use for midwestern deer. Which fly will the trout take best in April. The relative merits of rod materials. A better way to call turkeys. In this publishing market, style is too often secondary; the lack of it being excused by the value of ten hot tips. This all too often becomes writing only by virtue of being in print.

I have one widely published friend who's been quoted, in effect: "My readers don't care if I say them fish or those fish, as long as I tell them how to catch them fish." To a large extent, that's true. They don't care, and all my wishing that they would won't make it so. But I think my friend abuses his craft. To be widely published is to write almost constantly. It's an undisputable grind, within which it's much easier to subvert the imagination and discipline needed for a well-written story. It's a trap into which many have fallen, including, I admit, myself.

At the other extreme is much writing that conveys no information at all, but rather conveys—or attempts to—the experience. There are, I know, few things more glorious than having your son catch his first trout on a fly. I also know—and my optometrist will attest to it—the horrible strain of reading a manuscript that opens thusly: "It was Danny's first trout." Send it back. As far back as you can.

I have often wondered just what motivates good people to do these bad things. I surmise, of necessity, that they just don't know. Their prose is heartfelt, therefore it must be good. They have experienced something deep and wish to share it in print. Compounding this compulsive confessional (too many C's, John) is a literary tradition that encourages participation.

Hunting and fishing are both sports in which the participants become, by definition, authorities. Ask any fisherman. Ask any hunter. And be prepared to hear more than you want to know. Fly-fishing, for example, has generated a greater body of literature about itself than any other sport. For centuries, it was the sole province of nobility. As an educated upper-middle class developed, fly-fishing became theirs, together with an acquired taste for sport along with simple meat. In one respect, the evolution of fly-fishing and hunting in print has been a burgeoning of semiliterate egomaniacs eager to record their adventures. On the stream. On the hillside grouse coverts. In the deep woods. I have had not a few nightmares in which I've been treed at streamside by a manuscript-waving horde.

Fortunately, the role of *the experience* in writing about hunting and fishing hasn't been all bad, which also helps to make another point. One of the columnists for a major fly-fishing magazine is widely known for the gentle, nontechnical nature of his writing. He loses fish. He falls in rivers. He drops car keys and gets chased by bulls. He wouldn't presume to instruct, at least not overtly. His fumbling in print is accomplished with impeccable literary style; he is a fine writer, a conscientious stylist who works at his words. Year after year, and for all the how-to, good and bad, that also appears in the magazine, his column is consistently the most popular editorial feature. Them fish have never appeared within it.

One reason for the popularity of this particular writer, I'm certain, is that people can easily identify with what he says. Note again, however, that his midstream fumbling is done with writing that's both imaginative and technically solid. The topic allows readership identification, but without his superb writing skills there would be little readership. Simply to have experienced a trout stream or a grouse covert is not a license to literature. Few would-be hunting and fishing writers seem to understand this, even though it's as if I decided, having once been in an airplane, that I could fly one.

There are some men, including some in this book, who have made a career of writing about what they like best: The outdoors. From that association, not unique to them, certainly, evolved the term *outdoor writer,* which commonly describes hunting, fishing and conservation writers. The term itself is absurd. It might, taken literally, refer to all those writers who write out-of-doors. Please let me not be an outdoor writer. Writer, yes; outdoor, no.

One problem is that many writers in this so-called field have been outdoorsmen first and writers second. A woodcock thicket thus becomes thicker in print than in real life. Preposition Swamp claims yet another victim. There are notable exceptions, of course, such as Gene Hill and Frank Woolner, as represented in this book. They and a few others are at once fine outdoorsmen and fine writers, but the combination is all too rare.

I should set aside the shotgun and bring out what I earlier called a box of Band-Aids. Things aren't all bad, and perhaps I can highlight some things that will help readers to read and (some) writers to write. It has, for example, bothered me to hear someone say: "Sure, it's easy for you, 'cause you just knock those stories off with no trouble." 'Tain't so. They are, in truth, a lot of trouble.

Learning something about how writers write may make your own reading more enjoyable, or at least more appreciative. Most of the following is based partly on my own experience and also on dealing as an editor with many writers far better than I. A good story doesn't spring into being; it most often walks and sometimes crawls. I have paced office hallways, apparently doing nothing, for hours until I was able to declare the story done. All that remained was the writing.

Thinking a story through may take minutes or months. Many writers work that way, writing while they stare into space or mow the lawn. The actual writing often comes quickly, but it's also the iceberg's tip. Others do their thinking on paper. The bedside notepad kept ready for a midnight flash is one example, albeit cliché. Draft after draft, note upon note, changing a word and changing again—it's hard labor, mental and physical. In either case, the effort usually shows.

As one example, I offer John Voelker, better known under

his Robert Traver pen name. I must also explain that the editor/author relationship is something of a confessional: No editor who wishes to preserve his credibility will air his authors' dirty laundry. I tell this tale convinced that the complimentary point will justify the transgression. Which point is simply that Voelker works hard at his writing. A Voelker manuscript is edited carefully, if at all. The mail then brings a legal sheet marked with his revisions. A couple of days later, there will be more. And more. The man will literally pursue a better word to the presses. I wish I had both his perception and his discipline.

Thinking of Voelker takes me to another point, a knack which good writers strive to recognize and to develop and which readers applaud: Fresh phrasing. People of inherited wealth are those, by cliché, "born with silver spoons in their mouths." With great delight, I read a Voelker adaptation, used to describe a wealthy angling group as "sons of riches born with Silver Doctors in their mouths. . . ." Not only does he brighten the shopworn spoon, his play on words also conveys an apparent disdain, all in ten words. He will not, I hope, regard my interpretation as vandalism.

Consider another example, this time from the late Sparse Grey Hackle. Asked what to tell someone who wished to fish for trout, his answer was: "Tell them to fish for bass." Sparse's rapier strikes again, answering our overcrowded trout streams. And again I am envious, resolving to practice more with a rapier and less with an ax.

Something that few readers seem to appreciate, and which most competent writers know, is that a writer of an article or book has put a piece of himself on paper. It's a piece that once on paper is gone, not to return. Part of that piece is a sincerity of expression that's reflected in the printed page. It's a subtle thing, but an important one. Important because that sincerity has sometimes made a fishing or hunting writer great, even with a writing style that was merely competent. Ray Bergman, Joe

Brooks and Jack O'Connor were all fishing or hunting writers who reached and stayed at the top not only because their information was solid, but because they appeared as sincere in print. I did not know any of those men, and I wish that I had. My impression of their sincerity is lasting and produces that wish.

As an editor occasionally mired in mediocre manuscripts (too many M's, John), I often despaired at finding, for example, another Ray Bergman. Well, there won't be another Ray Bergman. A writer, after all, is nothing if not unique in some ways. But there are some truly fine young writers coming along for whose work you should watch. Once, while muddling in the mass of manila mail (M's), I came upon a Harrison O'Connor manuscript. (He also has a story in this anthology.) This was a number of years ago when he hadn't been published as widely as now, and it was, even then, striking. His style was unlike any writer I'd read in the field, and it was pleasing. There are a few developing writers in this book, but I single him out: First, as being among the younger ones and second, because his article falls in a generic how-to grouping, while at the same time it's uniquely written. In reading his story, try to read how he writes as well as what. You'll find it rewarding.

Unusual. Sincere. Genuine. Fresh. Accurate. Stylistically correct. All of those attributes have been assigned here to good writing. Judging a writing contest such as this one has been an education for me and, I suspect, for all those involved. Reading, then voting. Debating, and then voting again. And again, until we had our winners. The arguments in a closed room provided a crash course for anyone interested in writing. It is in some ways unfortunate that those discussions will remain locked away. But in a general sense, many of the things we discussed in judging, many of the criteria we used, have been cited here. I hope you think of them as you read. And I hope they add to your enjoyment of this book.

# Introduction

THE C. F. ORVIS WRITING CONTEST was established by The Orvis Company in 1981 "to promote excellence in writing that deals with fly fishing, bird hunting, and the conservation of fish and game species." For the first two years three categories were judged: best published magazine story exemplifying the sporting way of life as it pertains to bird hunting and/or fly fishing, best published magazine story concerning the conservation and/or management of fish and/or game species, best published "how to" fly fishing magazine article. For 1983 a fourth category was added: best published newspaper article on fly fishing.

I remember agonizing over the first year's entries in a stuffy hotel room during the 1982 Theodore Gordon Flyfishers' annual meeting. Fellow judges Nick Lyons, Paul Schullery, Perk Perkins, John Merwin and I had trouble reaching a consensus in a particular category. My favorite lost. Although the judging was certainly fair, I was disappointed—not only because I didn't get my way but because I felt the story deserved more recognition and a wider audience that it originally received.

You can now enjoy that story, and many others that almost won or were particular favorites of the judges. *The Orvis Anthology* is a distillation of what we feel is the best writing about hunting and fishing from the years 1981 and 1982. Unlike most anthologies, it doesn't contain just nostalgia or just articles on technique. There's some history here, some timely information on the management of our resources, how-to articles that entertain as well as instruct—plus a generous dose of nostalgia that is definitely a cut above the overworked "Grandpa and the Boy" theme.

If you can read the first story in this volume without getting a little choked up, you've never been owned by a hunting dog.

It's interesting and encouraging to note the diversity of the sources of these stories—from up-and-coming special interest publications like *Fly Fisherman* and *Rod & Reel* to established giants such as *Esquire* and *National Geographic*. And, of course, *Field and Stream* and *Sports Afield,* known for decades for their editorial integrity, are well represented.

It is the hope of The Orvis Company that the scope of this contest will continue to enlarge, and that in some small way it will encourage writers to concentrate on producing fine literature as well as good advice. Happy reading.

Tom Rosenbauer
Manchester, Vermont
January, 1984

# "One"

## Gene Hill

I ADMIRED THE DOG out of courtesy, and that was about it. He wasn't anything special to look at—just your nice, solid, big-headed black Lab. I've seen hundreds just like him, give or take an inch here or a detail there. His work in the field was efficient but not exciting. He wasn't what a real trial man would call steady, and as often as not, he'd drop a goose to re-adjust a hold, generally preferring to drag it along by a wing. He did have the peculiar habit of never picking up a bird, no matter how dead it was, without stepping on the bird's neck with one foot and holding it there until he'd grabbed the wing. I asked about this and his owner told me that his first goose had pecked him pretty badly. This bit of cause-and-effect reasoning pleased me, being a "once burned, twice shy" person myself.

That day in a goose pit on the Eastern Shore of Maryland was as common as the surrounding mud. Intermittent flights had us calling, more for the amusement of it than for any real hope of turning them. But every so often a pair or a small flock of five or six would toll close enough for a shot, and since we were in no hurry or really that anxious to take geese, we took turns with the gunning. By midafternoon we each had two geese, enough for our personal satisfaction. The weather was mild and we had come to a mutual, although unspoken, agreement to just sit there and chat rather than pick up and go our separate ways. It was a lovely way to spend an afternoon. Gunning talk mostly, a little fishing, some book titles exchanged—just your average smalltalk between two men who were relative strangers but found common ground and an occasional bit of laughter that sweetened the conversation and made each of us at ease and wanting the other to find us good company. It was a small, pleasant, spontaneous friendship.

He hardly mentioned his Lab nor did I, but I was pleased to notice that the dog sat leaning a little against his master's leg and put his head on his master's foot when he chose to lie down. My companion's hand was stroking the dog, and messing with his ears and scratching him behind the neck. Just the sort of thing any one of us might do, an ordinary circumstance, a commonplace relationship. Nor did I find it strange that the dog paid absolutely no attention to me whatsoever. There are dogs that are nuisances for affection (several of mine were like that from being spoiled and encouraged to play) and others that like to keep to themselves; and there are others that are clearly one-person creatures.

My companion had not bothered to bring a lunch, and I, for once, had gotten myself together and packed one. As usual, when I do get the lunch-making urge, I tend to go overboard, and I had more than enough to share, which I did gladly. We each had two sandwiches, and as my companion ate one he fed the other to his dog at the same pace, bite for bite. A sandwich and a half was enough for me, and I offered the dog the half left over. He wouldn't touch it from my hand, so I placed it on the floor of the blind in front of him where it sat unnoticed and untasted until I asked my companion if the dog was on some sort of self-imposed diet.

"No, I don't think so," he said with a laugh, and picked up the food and fed it to the dog bite by bite.

"Most Labs I know would have taken the thing in one bite and a lot would have threatened the hunting coat sleeve at the same time," I said.

"Well, we do things a little different, don't we?" my companion said, feeding the dog tiny wren-size crumbs in a playful manner.

You can usually sense when someone has been waiting for a chance to talk about something that needs to be aired. You feel that he's been looking for the right time and place and ear, and I was hoping that I'd have that privilege. So I just sat there and watched him dribble pieces of that sandwich, pieces about the size of OO buck, to a dog that was obviously not only used to this little game, but so delighted with it that he was making soft moaning noises and rolling his eyes like a Fundamentalist convert.

"This Pete here is about the worst dog I've ever owned," he said with some hesitation. "But he's taught me more about dogs, in a strange way, than most of the others I've had—and there have been quite a few."

I just sat there and stared at the floor of the blind, not wanting to look at him, because he didn't want to look at me. Right now he wanted a listener, a sympathetic and understanding one who had some knowledge of what he was talking about. But he didn't want a conversation. Just the ear would do fine for the time being.

"If you've ever followed the big field-trial circuit, you'd probably know my name," my companion said. "For quite a few years I was the amateur trainer that most of the pros worried about. And they had good reason. I had the money, the time, the drive, and the dogs. And you needed all that just to start because you were in against the Belmonts, the Roosevelts, and big steel money, big oil money, and just plain money so big that hardly anyone remembered where it all did come from. One handler drove his dogs to the trials in an old Rolls Royce fitted up like a kennel truck. The people he worked for drove Rolls and they didn't want their dogs in anything less! I didn't go that far, but I wasn't too far behind. I've chartered more than one plane to take my dogs where I thought they ought to be running, and I never regretted a penny.

"I even had Purdey make me a pair of side-by's just for gunning in a trial in case my dogs didn't finish, so I'd still be part of the action. You learn a lot about certain dogs when you're a gun—but that's getting away from my story.

"It all started simply enough, and typically, as far as I'm concerned. I've always loved competition. I've been a top flight amateur golfer and a tournament winner on the trap and skeet circuit, and I got to where they knew I was there in the live bird rings of Madrid and Mexico. Then I got thinking about getting a dog. I traveled so much in my early days that owning one didn't make much sense. My hosts when I went shooting all had fine kennels, so it didn't make any difference if I had any or not. In fact it was better that I didn't. But when a big holding company bought me out for more money than I could ever spend and moved me up to some spot that was all title and no work, I began to look around for something new to take up. It was just about destined that I'd start field trialing Labs.

"I'd been a member of one of those fancy Long Island duck clubs for years and had seen some pretty good dogs. It might sound silly, but I believe that a man has to have a dog and a breed of dog that suits his personality. If I believed in reincarnation I don't doubt that I'd come back as a Lab—or would like to. It's a little vain, but I saw myself as brave, hon-

4

est, and strong, as Hemingway might have put it, and that's what I like about the Lab. It's all up front, nothing held back.

"Anyway, one of my duck hunting buddies at the old Sprig Club had a litter of dogs out of good field trial stock, and he gave me a male as sort of a retirement present. He said that at worst he'd be somebody I could talk to and take care of and get the same in return. After I'd spent a few weeks with the pup I decided to have a professional take a look at him. I felt that he might have what it takes to be a trial dog, but I believe in the opinions of the people who do it every day, not just an amateur appraisal.

"THE PROFESSIONAL NOT ONLY LIKED the dog but made an offer then and there to take him for training, and I agreed. He had a fine reputation, and I liked his whole approach to the trialing idea. He was to start the dog, and when he was satisfied, I'd come down and spend a week or so with him and learn to run

the dog myself. Then I'd get a training schedule to work on and check back with him for a few days on a regular basis. If the dog did exceptionally well, the professional would take him over completely and campaign in the major stakes. His name was Wonderdog, because I wondered what I'd do with him when I first got him. If you followed the retrievers, you know how far he got, and what a piece of pure bad luck that he didn't become National Champion. He was killed a little while after his first National—an assistant trainer was in an accident and the dog trailer was totally demolished. I was hurt by the loss, of course, but by then I'd been committed to try for another dog as good as he was. He'd sired a litter and I arranged to get the pick for stud service.

"If anything, he was better than his father—a bit more aggressive and strangely a bit more biddable. It was almost as if he felt destined to compete and understood what was expected of him all along. I called him Little Wonder. Most everyone was soon calling him One, short for number one because that's what he looked like right from the start. He was one of the hottest derby dogs anyone had ever seen when he was right, and he usually was. I'd never thought of a dog as an athlete before, but when One took to the water, he reminded me of a gymnast or a diver—I know it's silly to think of a dog having 'form,' but he really did—and I somehow never got over the idea that he knew it and worked at it.

"By the time he was three, One had totally captivated the trial circuit. Not just in wins and placements, but with his personality and his pure competitiveness and genius for doing just the right thing at the right time. I know for sure that more than one judge laid out a series with just him in mind, but as hard as they tried to challenge him, he was usually up to it. Of course he had an off-day now and then, disinterested or bored or maybe tired, but even then he did his job, though without the fire he was famous for. In his first National at Bombay Hook he placed third. I don't think he deserved to win, but I think he deserved at least second. The head judge and I weren't exactly friends, since I'd beaten his dog at several important trials, and he wasn't above playing a little politics with some nationally known names.

"I'd planned to retire One after he won the Nationals, and just use him as a stud dog and my gunning companion. We'd become pretty close, and I thought he deserved a little rest and some fun. Some of the fun had gone out of the competition as far as I was concerned. But I did want that win for him in the worst way. He'd worked hard for it and most of us still believed that he had the class and the talent to go all the way. If any dog deserved it, One certainly did.

"The more we worked him that season, the sharper he got. I didn't think there was much room for improvement, but in subtle ways he just looked better. His long blinds were precision itself, and when he was stopped to the whistle he really *stopped*. It was as if he were reading your mind—I heard one judge remark in a friendly way that he looked as if he were showing off. I'm making him sound as if he was absolutely perfect, but he did have one small fault. Every so often—not in every trial—for some reason he'd make one or two little yelps on a land retrieve. I always put it down as pure enthusiasm, and the trainer and I had long given up trying to make him stop it. More often than not, we'd be the only ones to notice it."

Here my companion paused for so long I didn't think he was going to go on with the rest of the story. He was rumpling his dog and searching for the right words and the strength to say them. I had the feeling that this was a story he'd never told before and perhaps didn't want to tell now, yet knew that he must so he could get a different grip on it himself. For some strange reason I thought of the words to an old song about "hanging your tears out to dry"—how perfectly put, how perfectly true.

For the first time since he'd begun, he turned to look at me and I could see the gray, sad sparkle of small tears. I turned a bit away to give him a moment of privacy. He covered his face with his handkerchief for just a second, and then he went on.

"I'D SAY THE ODDS on what happened were more than one in a million. It was one of those random tragedies that seem always to strike the innocent, the casual passerby. There was a strand of wire, just one, that was only about 2 feet long between an old post and a tree. I'd heard One making his odd yipping noise and suddenly he went end over end in the air and lay still. Both the judges and I rushed out, knowing that something fearful had happened. There was One, stretched out, dead from a broken neck. Small trickles of blood ran down the corners of his jaws where he'd run into the wire with his mouth open.

"I carried him back to the station wagon and put him on the front seat and started to drive. I don't remember how long or where I went, but I do remember that I kept rubbing his head, believing for the longest time that he'd suddenly sit up and everything would be all right. Today was the second time in my life that I've ever cried. The day One died was the first.

"There's a small graveyard behind the lodge at the Sprig Club where that special dog would be put to rest. The whole club turned out to help me put One there. I had a blanket made of his ribbons and my gunning coat was his pillow. He always loved to sleep on that whenever he had the chance. One of the members read a list of his wins. Then he paused, and in a soft tenor began to sing Auld Lang Syne. Everyone, except me, joined in."

My companion stopped again for a minute and blew his nose. I must confess I did the same.

"I virtually stopped gunning for a long time after that,"

he continued. "When people asked me why, I told them that my favorite partner had passed away. Almost none of them ever thought that it might have been my dog. Funny, isn't it, how few can understand the relationship a man can have with his dog? And yet I can tell you now that there were few, if any, things in my life that meant as much to me as One. How odd but true that an emptiness like that is there forever.

"It's been about five years since I lost One, and last fall a friend of mine, the same one that sang that afternoon at the duck club, came to my house and rang the bell. When I opened the door he reached in and put a puppy in my arms and said: 'It's about time Pete had someone to look after.' This is Pete."

At the sound of his name Pete looked up and made some sort of a face that I'd say was as close to smiling as a dog can get.

"When I said that Pete was the worst of my dogs I meant that I'd never trained him. I just let him be Pete. And that's been enough, more than enough. They say that a man deserves one good dog in his life, but that's not true. I've had a couple, and in his own way Pete's right there in my heart with them all now. It's a full space with two empty ones beside it if you can see it that way."

I nodded to let him know that I agreed, but I didn't say anything because I didn't think anything needed saying just at the moment.

He began, after a little while, to talk about something else, and after giving me his card, he thanked me for listening and said it was time for him and Pete to be heading on home. I said goodbye and told him that I'd wait here a little while longer in the blind just to watch the sun come down. But that wasn't the whole truth. What I wanted to do was sit there in the quiet of twilight and hear the soft phrases of that ancient Scottish melody again in my mind and picture the scene of that group of men singing a dog to eternity and comforting themselves in the timeless ritual of shared sorrow and understanding of loss.

In the last light I slung my two geese over my shoulder and started back to where I'd left the car. I found myself softly singing what I could remember of One's funeral song, and surprisingly I wasn't as saddened by the idea as you'd imagine. The saving thought was one of remembrance; as long as a man lives, so will his dogs live in one form or another in a story or a song. I can't think of a nicer way to put it than that we will "share a cup of kindness now. . . ." §

# The Pheasant-Tail Nymph

*Harrison O'Connor*

BECAUSE I BECOME much more motivated when I can hunt for and cast to sighted fish, I have sought a specialized form of trout fishing, one so compelling that it has stunted my growth as a fisherman. Inevitably I have gone to spring creeks. And there I have found the fishing of which I never tire: stalking along, observing the trout, casting a nymph to the ones I wanted to catch. This is, of course, the method of fishing popularized by that famous English riverkeeper, the late Frank Sawyer, a tall man with good eyes who found that he could catch most any trout by pitching one of his pheasant-tail nymphs well upstream of the fish, then watching as the quick-sinking fly drifted down to the trout, gently setting the hook after he saw the inside of the trout's mouth flashing white when the unsuspecting fish turned to take the fly. Without any hesitation I can say that the most important trout fly that I carry is Sawyer's pheasant-tail. As to its effectiveness, I need only to refer to the last entry in a notebook recounting a recent month-long trip to the West.

(It was early September, and we had camped near Idaho's Henrys Fork for ten days. One night a tremendous lightning storm seemed to surround us, the flashing so bright, the bolts striking so near that I could not look out of the tent. With my head on the ground I could feel the lightning strike, seemingly, deep into the ground. Such a night made us all feel closer and fonder of morning—the sagebrush so bright-lit and the river always steaming—and the pleasant routine into which we had settled. Camping so close to the water, I knew that there was little insect activity at dawn. At midmorning, some small duns began to emerge, followed by a fall of spinners if the wind didn't blow them off the river, followed by a long period of slow feeding when ants worked well and pheasant-tails worked better.)

Woke up on this very warm morning feeling extremely still and intolerant of noise, even of spoons banging. Fishermen began to arrive, more than I have ever seen down here, about a dozen. But I wanted pancakes and tea and didn't budge. Sipped slowly. Even promised Levin (three years old) that I would help him cast before going on my own. He had demanded that I rig up his own fly rod now that the older boys were fly-fishing. I tarried because the last couple of days hadn't been much—the morning hatch windspoiled, and the evening hatch of miniature duns of no consequence.

But as I approached the water I saw that it was a much better morning than I had anticipated. I could see the silvery swarms of dancing spinners, and on the water, the wings of small blue duns as well as large, chalky spinners, midges—everything. Only a slight breeze stirred.

Then I knelt in front of Levin and looked into his very serious, brown eyes, begging him to let me try for that one fish before our casting lesson. He nodded soberly and sat down in the meadow with the authority of an Indian chief, not to be ignored, freeing me to wade carefully into the water well upstream of the riser. Slowly I eased downstream into position, stepping closer only when the fish rose, and remarking to myself: What luck! All these fishermen had ignored this quiet, shallow bay where for years a few big fish have been wont to cruise. Waiting for the trout to rise again I listened to the fishermen. "Fish a number twenty Adams on 7X," said one. Now I felt I had exactly the right flies for this morning's fishing. I would start with a small emerger/floating nymph, just a little bit of wing breaking out of the wingcase, that I had tied with mole fur, and I would switch to a spinner pattern when the trout turned on to the spinner.

But I could not catch one fish, not one. All the while the voices continued.

A woman called, "Hooked and lost one on a Wulff!" Jesus. Another man responded, "Actually hooked one on a size 12 Royal Wulff." How can that be? The little duns were a size 20. Another man suggested, "Try a small goofus." Well, the fish took it for a cripple. I was more than exasperated, I was finished. Finally I tied on a size 20 pheasant-tail and twice saw the leader tick forward, but I was in a slump and did not react.

I waded out of the river and said to Moira, who was trying her best to deal with Levin, "Let's get out of here. Fish down at my spot." What I was really saying was: Can't fish and listen to these people. My spot really meant my way of fishing.

I had found a 200-yard stretch of shoreline, rocky and pebbly and shallow and slow—and so illuminated by the morning sun that I could sight-fish, never casting until I saw the waving tail of a good fish. I believe I had pricked, at least, every trout along this shoreline. There seemed to be a dozen 18-inchers feeding in the shallows. I had lost one tremendous trout that bolted and turned around at my feet as the hook pulled out. I had caught a four-pounder and a couple weighing three pounds. All on pheasant-tails. I began fishing this shore-line when, during a good hatch, I had noticed a particularly interesting riseform. Watching carefully I saw that the fish nymphed a dozen times for every time that he rose. I hooked and lost the fish in the weeds and, on my way upstream, startled other big fish, noting their heavy wakes as they swam to mid-stream. By repeatedly fishing this shoreline I eventually learned the feeding lies of the fish, and I began to succeed.

"Now bear with me," I told Moira; meaning, here I can catch fish.

When I turned to face the river, I heard an odd noise and turned back to see her sticking her tongue out at me.

"At least you've smiled, finally," she said.

I had been a bit sour. But not now. Here was a good place to fish, with no fishermen around. Immediately I spotted a very dark fish. Old with age, I said to myself. Gradually I eased closer, confident because of the trout's dark, sickly color. I had often fished for such oldies on the Letort; the dark ones always seem to be in a stupor, so much so that they are reluctant even to bolt. I could see this was a nice fish, but I stepped closer, sure of myself because I could see a white wound and presumed

that the fish was blind on my side. I began casting, pitching little more than the leader. No response. I've got to put the fly right on the bottom, right in front of his nose, I reasoned, so I switched to Sawyer's Killer Bug, a real sinker. But I could see that the light-colored fly was not reaching bottom. I sensed that even a large wet fly would not frighten this stuporous fish. On went a dark caddis pupa, so heavily weighted that I could see ribs of lead under the dubbing. I plunked it ahead of the fish. Suddenly he came to life, raising slightly and gulping. I tightened up to him confident that he wouldn't fight hard. I had a long 6X tippet. Around and around I led the fish until I could get a hand around him. He was 21½ inches long, in excellent condition despite his dark color, with a superficial wound on his gill plate. His eyes were fine. This was a good fish! Happily, I began to fish again. And there right in front of me an even bigger trout moved greedily to catch a nymph. Lordy. But I felt totally calm.

"This one will really go!" I called to Moira, because I could see this was a beautiful colored, healthy trout feeding decisively, in a way that made me feel that the fish was confident, but on edge.

And casting my last pheasant-tail, of dozens that I had purchased from Sawyer after reading his book many years ago—but it would be years before I began to fish these flies properly—I saw the fish take. On the strike it surged forward, as big fish will, not in panicked rush, but swimming nervously upstream seemingly determined to outdistance this well-known nuisance, the fisherman, who could be broken off. My rod pointed straight at the fish, I hurried after him so as to keep as little tension as possible. I wanted this fish to believe he could swim away from the problem and to wear himself down before the inevitable explosion occurred. When I heard myself say, how I want this fish, I woke up and eased off all tension. Whenever I hear or feel myself wanting a fish, I know I am unconsciously tightening up—it's like hearing the humming of a monofilament line that is about to break—and I adopt the attitude that I don't really care what happens. So I pretend that this fish really doesn't matter, not too convincingly.

The trout swam worriedly upstream (good, wear yourself down, I said to myself), now turning this way and that, its head ticking irritably, now suddenly spinning and thrashing wildly, now diving under weed. Once it jumped. We wandered two-thirds of the way across the river to a waist-deep channel. I felt slightly relieved, knowing that in deep water I could control the fish more easily. Finally I pulled the trout back by me, saw it clearly, and suffered another attack of wanting. If I just had a net I'd get this fish. In that thought there was no consolation. I eased off and followed the trout, leaning on him with as much pressure as I dared.

At last my two hands were around her, for the trout was a lovely hen fish, which I carried back to Moira for photos. She measured 24 inches long. Rather than bother her any further, I snapped off the fly in her mouth, and away she swam, in good shape.

For good measure I promptly caught one more, 18 inches long, then quit. Enough. Now I am back in camp, with a cup of tea, feeling so completely satisfied that I am conscious of feeling heavy and slow and calm and sure of myself.

That feeling lasted all day; in the evening I did not fish, but sat above the river watching a rise of fish and listening to the fussing of ducks.

WHILE AT FIRST SIGHT the fly may inspire little confidence, fishing the pheasant-tail nymph will instill in one skepticism for complicated fly patterns, a desire for similar, clean-silhouetted, quick-sinking, all-purpose caddis and stonefly imitations, a confirmed belief in the efficacy of deep, dead-drifted wet flies, and a slight boredom with heavy-handed methods of catching big fish. Can it be that this simple fly, only a thinly disguised hook with a wingcase on its back, can reduce trout fishing in spring creeks, where supposedly the trout are fussiest, to but one fundamental concern: a desire for proper presentation? Much of the day, yes.

I learned the "pitching game" on the Letort, where the uniformity of trout behavior resulting from living in a stream absolutely choked by sedimentation and plants, makes the fishing unique.

At these feeding stations the trout concentrate upon the fisherman, having seemingly learned that he follows certain paths, wears bright clothes, casts repetitiously and prefers certain flies. In order to defend themselves against his attacks, the trout adopt a definite pattern of feeding marked by long, staring pauses interrupted by the occasional, seemingly listless lunge forward to grab yet another cress bug. This extremely deliberate style of feeding is not so much disinterest in a monotonous diet as it is the conditioned slow motion of a trout feeling extremely self-conscious in still, shallow water far from his hiding hole.

The Letort fisherman may learn little about entomology and less about distance fly-casting, but he must become an effective stalker of skittish fish and a good judge of a trout's moods in order to know when and how often he can safely present the fly. The notion that a trout sees less as its cone of vision diminishes, when it rises from the deep to feed near the surface, brings the fisherman little comfort as he flushes trout after trout holding in inches of water. Soon he is crawling into position, kneeling in the tall grass, watching a trout that is holding in a pocket of dead water on the near side of the stream, not thirty feet upstream. The trout is barely finning. The fisherman has learned that passivity in a trout is the mood to respect. So he waits for the fish to drop his guard, for the fins to activate and for the head to tick greedily as the trout commences to hunt along the edge of the cress.

When a brown trout of the Letort has relaxed into a groove of careful feeding, its tail will flap out of the water as it nudges forward to pin down a cress bug. The trout will tail at regular intervals. It may adopt a definite beat, feeding up the alley between a cress bed and the shoreline to its dead end, then turning, gliding back to the starting position to begin again after another long, watchful pause. The more adamantly that a trout turns its head, then scoots to catch a shrimp, displaying confidence gained from a long period of unmolested feeding, the more likely that the fish can be caught. The voracious feeders (if a trout of the Letort can ever be said to feed voraciously) can be cast to at a pace about equal to the frequency of their tailing.

But the habitually cautious trout must be offered the fly at so deliberate a pace that his suspicion, so easily aroused, eventually subsides until, hopefully, he takes. It is often said that a trout's willingness to take a fly is reduced by each successive cast. The Letort fisherman learns to wait long enough between casts that each presentation is essentially a first cast. He delivers his pitch when the trout is in the act of feeding. The fly line lands on the cress and the leader on the water, the tippet piling up, releasing a size 20 wet fly to drift, unfettered by any drag, in this dead water slowly down to the fish. If the fly is not noticed or is refused, the line is picked up when again the fish is in the act of feeding. If the trout ever backs down the alley, a sure sign that he is about to bolt, he must be rested. I have written in such detail about Letort fishing because it is the foundation of my approach to nymph fishing for sighted trout.

Exactly this tempo—a cautious trout nymphing occasionally, an observant fisherman casting correspondingly slowly, having chosen a fly whose sink rate matches the current and depth of water, pitching it only when the fish is relaxed—characterizes typical pheasant-tail nymph fishing. The morning I described on the Henrys Fork is a good example. A multiple hatch of flies had stirred up the trout. The hatching had subsided. There were still flies on the water, and the little fish could be heard blipping regularly. But now the sun was bright on the water. Though the bigger fish were still in feeding lanes, they felt loath to move, rising infrequently if at all, but willingly gulping any nearby nymph. Enter the pheasant-tail.

Inevitably one must ask, why is it that a good-size, experienced trout will take a pheasant-tail much larger than the nymphs on which it is feeding—and take the fly as unconsciously as a commuter reaching into a bag for yet another potato chip—yet will exercise utmost care when scrutinizing a floating artificial matching the duns on which it is also feeding? Of course, trout will key to the size of both the nymphs and the duns when a strong hatch is in progress, but during times of slow feeding when the fish are in secure lies, it has been my experience, fishing pheasant-tails, often in a size 14 in order to reach the bottom, that the trout are not particularly critical of sunken flies, yet they can be seen to visibly concentrate upon floating patterns.

I have knelt close behind Letort browns and watched them come to life, activating their fins, at the thought of rising to an ant, but refusing to do so, I believe, out of reluctance to move so boldly as to rise, then moments later, gulping down a cress bug without showing a flicker of concern. And I have watched the trout of one Virginia limestone stream during the first season that stream was opened to fishing. All the fishermen were fishing hoppers, seeing the trout rise up under live grasshoppers and drift back just inches under the real insect only to refuse. Yet the same trout would take my nymph. These are fish that have been punished by fishermen.

The habit of selectivity in a trout is activated, at least in part, for two reasons: the need to conserve energy, and the need to protect itself. As rising to a fly on the surface is more energy consuming than taking a nearby nymph, and as it is a trout's natural instinct, from its fingerling days on, not to want to give away its position and therefore to prefer to move as little as possible when feeding, and as most fly fishermen habitually fish dry flies and, therefore, the majority of a fish's bad experiences with a hook result from rising, the arrival of a dry fly in a trout's window is likely to ring a bell—do I want this one? Often, Sawyer's nymph will not ring that bell.

For that reason, on hard-fished waters, the fly is invaluable. For two years running I have arrived on Nelson's Spring Creek, tied a small pheasant-tail onto a long, fine tippet, and immediately began catching fish. In both cases, the fish were not actively feeding—a few were rising at a pace typical of terrestrial feeding, others rolled over the occasional nymph—and my little fly drifting by did not frighten them however many times I cast. Inevitably I caught some.

As a hatch develops I often continue fishing a pheasant-tail about one size larger than the size of the emerging dun. I may fish through most of the hatch without having to change the fly, watching for the leader to zip forward after casting it ahead of a riser. But if I am confronted by a good fish locked into rising, I will first offer a floating nymph, then finally a dun, believing that a trout feels he is showing himself less taking the floating nymph than the dun.

As a matter of fact, when you fish a little pheasant-tail, say a size 20, you are essentially fishing a floating nymph. Over on Armstrong's Spring Creek in late October I had been having difficulty and felt myself tightening up, when by good fortune a hatch of size-20 blue duns came off, a hatch in which the nymphs must have been exceedingly vulnerable, because every trout in the stream locked into taking nymphs—they could be seen lined up in rows turning their heads this way and that.

Suddenly the fishing became a comedy. On every cast, I at least moved or pricked a fish with a size-20 pheasant-tail; in a couple of hours I landed many. I recall that twice I had waded out too far, was about to flood my waders, turned and floundered back through the muck, only to feel the rod over my shoulder come alive with a fish that had taken a trolled fly.

The most difficult and therefore the most rewarding way to fish a pheasant-tail is to try to catch trout lying on the bottom of deep channels, a skill at which Sawyer excelled and for which he designed his nymph series. All the fishing that I have described took place in water less than two-and-a-half feet deep. Only once that I can recall have I ever measured up to Sawyer's standard and felt that he might be looking down on me with a brief smile of approval. It was in New Zealand.

The South Island is a paradise, even today, for the fisherman who likes to walk many miles alone stalking the odd, big trout. I had a month's practice pitching nymphs ahead of big trout—on the Mataura, a friend and I walked along the pebbly beaches spotting swirls in very shallow water, casting small pheasant-tails and striking at the swirl; on the glacial blue mountain streams of Fiordland Park where skittish trout cruised shorelines, I had to cast where I thought the fish might arrive, then wait, watching for any odd movement or turn of the trout's head. At the end of my trip I reached Hokitika and looked up the local undertaker, who was said to be a good fisherman, finding the small, thin, freckled man in a pub surrounded by swarthy New Zealanders. He promptly directed me to a spring creek.

I have never seen the like; it was consistently four- to six-feet deep, its currents were violent, so the stream was spotlessly clean. I could, of course, see the trout; they ranged from three to five pounds. To give you some idea of the force and complexity of the current, I found myself lengthening and lengthening my tippet as a trout repeatedly rushed for, then refused, my dragging fly, a floating nymph that matched the very dark fly that was sporadically hatching. When the tippet became finally eight feet long, I caught the trout. That length of leader, piled up in a puddle cast, allowed the fly to float freely across the boiling current.

Then it began to rain, and the hatching of flies ceased. It became a very dark day of misting rain. I fished about a mile of stream three times, which is to say, I fished the stream badly, then a little better, and, finally, properly. On my first trip I located, by frightening them, the fish that were holding deep in the long pools. They could be seen idly nymphing between sparse weed beds. I caught none. On my second trip down my beat I persisted, changing locations, until I at least proved to myself that I could present a fly at that depth, even if I couldn't catch the fish. Fortunately the misting rain concealed me, and on my third trip I went from fish to fish, landing half a dozen good trout that each gave me a wonderful moment of pleasure, that moment when they turned so casually to gulp the pheasant-tail nymph that I had been praying all the way down to them.

Where ever you may fish—regardless whether you happen to be blasting away with a Royal Wulff on your favorite mountain stream and by chance the sun illuminates a corner of the pool revealing the biggest trout of your life—when you feel the need for an unfrightening fly, tie on a pheasant-tail, casting it well above the fish in a combination of a puddle and reach cast; then watch that fly steal past the trout's security system and into its mouth. §

# Praise the Grouse

*Frank Woolner*

I T WAS THE LAST DAY of an upland shooting season, ear-pinching cold with 2 inches of snow crunching underfoot. Hunting alone and without a dog, I meandered down to a little swamp, half-locked in ice. Black alders graced the edges, berries gleaming like rubies; below were a lot of high summer weeds stricken by New England's first hard winter offensive.

Later than late, really, since autumn was done and day was done. Light was fading, streaming out of a setting sun that glimmered through a western bank of poisonous green cloud. Wind tomorrow, and colder still, so this was the end of it. I thought a grouse might be there, and he was!

Moving forward without pause, I halted at a predetermined spot. It's an old jump-shooter's trick, for ruffed grouse will lie close if one maintains a steady cadence in approach, halting only when some long-trained and subconscious hunch says, *this is where he ought to be*. Pa'tridges, as we call them in our often hostile north country, may let a man walk right past without flushing, yet any abrupt halt seems to spell predator! Up he goes!

Of course I was swinging with the first battering of wings, roughly tracking by sound before the bird became visible above that shadowed tarn of seer brush, planning to compensate a split second later. He was a big cock, and a red-ruff too. It was almost a straight-away climbing shot, just a mite of deflection and swing-through.

A curious thing happened, something that had never happened to me before. I'm no Puritan or eco-freak, but suddenly it seemed impossible to press a trigger!

So I just tracked him, and it might have been an easy poke, and that was all. I shucked three shells out of a light auto-loader and went home. What difference did it make? Nobody was there to jeer and declare that I'd choked. It was just me and the bird in on this one.

Somehow, in those shaved seconds, it seemed only proper to say goodbye and good luck. Likely some convolution of an alleged brain sent an aboriginal message. Time for armistice! Let him drum in a burgeoning springtime and produce a whole phalanx of warriors for the golden aisles of autumn. A good thing is always better ended well.

Later that evening a close friend, who unfortunately never learned to hunt, asked how I'd done. Is it possible to explain so strange and magical an incident? It was enough to add a bit of scotch to the dregs still in a squat, crystal glass and say: "Nothing. Never fired."

Certainly anyone who admits a love affair with a gamebird may be, in the eyes of muddled colleagues, ready for commitment. There are good and true sportsmen who worship at the shrines of quail and pheasant. Good luck to them. Trouble is, I grew up in grouse country and it is my stubborn prerogative to insist that no other gamebird in the world is so great a challenge as this fan-tailed strategist.

Back when all of the world was young and kids learned to drive motor vehicles by chugging around home pastures in Model-T Fords, a few former market hunters still battled the brush. The tales they told were delicious, and every saga centered on pa'tridge or woodcock, the upland birds they had cut their teeth on. As a sidebar, when pheasants finally made an appearance, those lean, weather-worn ancients regarded them with scorn. "Nawthin' but tame chickens," they'd growl.

Perhaps one's beginnings remain ever-sacred, a nostalgia compounded of bright uplands in October, the heady scent of burnt powder and frustration as brown missiles went scaling through the trees to safety. Lord knows whether youngsters were supposed to buy licenses then, but nobody ever seemed to bother a farm boy up on the tangled slope of a side hill, armed with a single-barreled Sears & Roebuck scattergun, escorted by a wise family pointer—who probably went along for exercise and knew very well that no birds would be brought to account unless they were ground-hogged off a stone wall.

It takes a considerable passage of years before any gunman becomes even reasonably expert at racking down flying grouse. However, learning the necessary skills as a youth is better than a Thanksgiving dinner or salmon and peas on the Fourth of July. Laggard scholars who play hooky to go hunting soak up instruction and experience with an avidity schoolteachers would like to have directed elsewhere. Our pa'tridge was quite simply the greatest treasure imaginable.

After a lot of autumns in the uplands I still feel that the ruffed grouse never contributes to a boring moment on its own rough stamping ground. When, possibly lucky, you hit the first one in a shooting career and it goes slanting down ahead of a smoke trail of downy feathers, something exquisite has been accomplished. Moreover, no matter how long the fates allow a shooting man to exist, that exaltation remains.

First or last, it is always a miraculous triumph, a quick lightning flash of awe, a trembling climax. *By God, I really got him!*

In classic grouse cover a man or a woman (some women get just as entranced as the hairy-chested male animals) will find it is necessary to walk hard over some of the choppiest country ever created by scouring glaciers, possibly having clothing torn by clutching briars.

It never bothers me to meet a young, modishly clad hunter in my home coverts; but a flat-bellied, lean old-timer whose garb is scratched to hell and gone and whose wrists are crisscrossed with briar scratches bears watching. Inevitably the man will have an apparently gentle, philosophical pointer or setter at heel, the dog only straying scant yards away to piddle on an interesting stump.

If, having exchanged polite greetings and parted, later I hear a single shot down on an alder edge or up on a birch slope where barberries cluster in understory, I have an excuse for silent cussing. Rapid doubles or triples invariably mean that a bird has been missed. Surely there is much to be said for sharing, but I have never known a serious shooter who was fond of meeting an obvious shark in a hot corner he thought was his alone.

It is unwise to say that a pheasant towering out of an open swale swamp or cornfield like a helicopter with a broken rotor blade is an easy mark, but—there, I said it. To compound the insult, let me add that it doesn't seem to me that any quail buzzing over a thatch of low vegetation presents a very difficult target. To partially dress wounds, a bobwhite in thick cover can be just as tricky as a grouse, sometimes more so. I still prefer fan-tail, if only because he's nearly completely unpredictable and infuriatingly sagacious.

Beginners are always shocked out of their pants by the thunderous flush of a ruffed grouse. Many, often budding experts at skeet or trap, just stand there open-mouthed and mesmerized. It doesn't seem possible to hit such a hipper-dipper rocket, and there's no time to calculate. Everything happens rapidly. Nobody places his feet carefully, mounts a gun to shoulder, and yells "Pull!"

Veterans are never so handicapped by instant emotion, yet they also feel a strong surge of adrenaline every time a pat bores out, clattering through a screen of twigs, twisting, turning at apparently supersonic speed. The difference between a tyro and an experienced hand is that the latter works almost instinctively; he doesn't figure lead at all, but it is there nonetheless in a rapid swing-through. Snap-shooting is a term worthy of argument, since nobody ever killed a swiftly curving grouse by shooting right at it. The split-second deal is an optical illusion.

What really happens is that a quick marksman keeps his gun moving, sweeps right through the target and, although he may not know it himself, places a shot string just far enough ahead so that there will be interception at an instant in time and space. There are subtle nuances. It is obviously necessary to point above a rapidly towering bird, below if it happens to be diving, and there isn't time to whip out a slide rule to figure precise degrees. That has to be programmed inside a human headbone and locked into the aforementioned poke that has become instinctive through considerable experience.

Personally, I miss more "sucker shots," the straight-away flyer that should be elementary, than I do a wildly curving mark where deflection shooting is always required. Straightaways are missed because of over-lead and, often, over-confidence. There, a fast shooter tends to over-swing when all appears to be roses.

Two specific shots are hard to reckon with. One is the grouse that boils out of a tree overhead and goes slanting down in a sort of crash dive. All of our instinct screams for the rising lead, so the correct choice—to instantaneously shoot *under*—can take a beating. If this is not done, one stands in a whispering wilderness wreathed in the aromatic smoke of smokeless powder, sans fluffy feathers drifting.

The other is a pat that drives straight at your head. This can happen at any time, but is most likely when a companion flushes a bird and yells warning. Suddenly this bird is drilling right at you, and you see all of it at close range, feathers slicked back, eyes glittering, and wings a blur.

Textbook tactics call for a swift about-face and a quick shot going away. Unfortunately for you, and fortunately for the pat, excitement as this feathered missile whips by within inches of a sweating forehead induces undignified stumbling and off-balance, desperate shooting. Only the coolest of marksmen score regularly.

One day I guffawed as Hal Lyman, publisher of *Salt Water Sportsman* and therefore my boss, blew one I'd pushed right into him. Hal's an excellent scattergunner and he has harried gamebirds all over the world, but in relatively open cover he swiveled and threw two impotent charges at a rapidly disappearing target. His Scottish pointer, used to better things, almost sneered.

The greatness of ruffed grouse lies not alone in their ability to dodge at high speed, to bank around a protecting tree like a racing car rounding a pylon, or to scare you half to distraction by flushing at the most inopportune moment when one foot is in a mud hole and the other seeks a grip on a slippery, moss-draped boulder.

Please do not instruct me that it's easier to go in on solid point, for this can be most traumatic. Now you're psyched, tense, and jittery. Shooting glasses tend to cloud up as salt sweat trickles into bugging eyes. Nature holds its breath, and, for an agonizing yet blissful moment, it is still one against one. Combat may be thrilling, but there's considerable strain in moving up to the jump-off line.

Best of all, the grouse is completely wild; so far, rearing the bird in captivity has proved impossible. Born free, a stubborn American, no pa'tridge bows and scrapes before humankind. Push him back from one brushy hillside with industrial development, and he'll only retire to the next hill. The harder he's hunted, the warier he becomes.

But there's more than that. It is necessary to sweat and glory in a mite of pain tolerance in order to shoot these birds with any degree of success. It's hard work, meant for people who aren't entranced by an easy road to paradise, the "chicken farms" where pheasants are released the night before a hostile dawn.

Aside from the ego-deflating surprise tactics employed by grouse, they please me for other reasons, one being my own comfort. No need to arise before first light cracks in the east. Mornings at seven may have been right for Robert Browning, but our fall edges are likely to be frost-rimed and crispy then, far from dew-pearled. Fortunately for those of us who often work at night and are slug-a-beds at the birth of a new day, pats begin to forage most ardently after the sun is well above an eastern horizon. By that time a gunner can discard woolens and perspire gently under a light flannel shirt and shell jacket.

Basic guidelines apply, yet there is no royal road to success, for each pat is a rugged throwback to the birds of pioneer

America. Some patter along well ahead of dog or man to flush wild, towering over the trees beyond range of an open-bored shotgun. You stand there, bemused, frustrated, yet glowing with secret admiration for so crafty a bundle of feathers.

Rarely will a grouse do precisely what you expect him to do. One may flush right under your feet after you've relaxed and decided that a covert is barren. Another waits until such time as he can batter out behind a passing shooter, again necessitating the quick about-face that so often spells disaster.

There are always birds that come bombing out just when a gunner is fighting some jungle of grape vines, birch whips, or tangled alder. It's like being handcuffed at a banquet! One curses silently as a magnificent flyer towers so close at hand that you can can see every subtle etching of plumage, gleaming eyes, and the long, black-barred fan-tail spread in a climbing turn. Clutching brush defeats a quick and accurate swing, so there's nothing to do but cry inwardly after that wonderful bird is long gone, clipping through the twigs.

There are moments of fury and other occasions when it is pleasant to take a ten-minute break and rest, to lean one's weary back against a gnarled tree trunk at the edge of a forgotten orchard, to drink in the incomparable beauty of foliage brilliant with the last hectic fever of autumn, to nibble on a windfallen Baldwin apple, which is the spiciest of all fruit after a couple of hard frosts.

One cannot help savoring the pungent sweet and rotten perfume of a countryside still unpolluted by the ravages of that which is called progress, to relax under a high blue arch of sky with no alien racket of commerce other than the distance-muted groaning of a truck cranking over a remote cement ribbon or the lofty sigh of a jet plane bearing supposedly sophisticated passengers to neon-lighted pleasure places of the world.

Those poor folk don't know what they're missing right out in the back forty! §

# The Numbers Game

*George Reiger*

PESSIMISM AND CYNICISM are not the same thing. The Merriam-Webster dictionary and I agree on that point, but from slightly different perspectives.

The dictionary says a cynic is "one who believes that human conduct is motivated wholly by self-interest." I tend to call that person enlightened. For me, a cynic is a disillusioned idealist.

Most of his biographers agree that Abraham Lincoln was pessimistic, but not cynical, although he believed that "human conduct is motivated by self-interest." According to one story, he was stressing to a friend that altruism is a form of hypocrisy when the carriage in which they were riding passed a pig stuck in the middle of the muddy road. Lincoln ordered the carriage to stop, got down, and in his finest go-to-Congress clothes, wrestled the pig from the mud.

When his friend recovered from his laughter, he told Lincoln that if altruism was a form of hypocrisy, what was Lincoln doing helping the pig in the mud?"

"Acting selfishly," replied Lincoln. "I would have wondered all the rest of the day what had happened to the pig. Now I know."

A pessimist may have what the dictionary calls a "distrustful view of life in general and of the future," but he often retains many of the illusions the cynic has lost. That is why I am a pessimist, and not a cynic. I still have illusions about finding solitude, peace, and understanding in the great outdoors, and I even retain illusions about the meaning and value of those overused words. But I am pessimistic because instead of those values, I too often see competition, conspicuous consumption, and ignorance in the field and on the stream.

Ultimately I am a pessimist not because I believe Armageddon is imminent, but for precisely the opposite reason: because I believe that man will somehow survive each one of his Seven Deadly Sins, but live in a world of expectation vastly diminished from the one our grandfathers dreamed for us.

I once sat in a Southern diner with another outdoor writer and a press representative for the Army Corps of Engineers. The Corps man was trotting out statistics about how many more "recreational user days" (I think that was the lugubrious phrase he used) the local dam had created than had existed before, when the river flowed freely and produced only charging channel cats and feisty smallmouth bass. Behind us, two fishermen were arguing about whether canned corn was better than frozen corn as trout bait.

The Corps' representative talked so much about launch ramps and marinas that my colleague asked whether there was any place left for an angler to get off by himself—to wade and to cast. "Yes," said the Corps man triumphantly. "There are two parking areas from which we've cut trails to the lake so poor people without boats can canepole for crappie."

He paused and then confessed. "But we've had some trouble with litter, and two weeks ago, a couple of boys were beaten up and robbed by a gang of hoodlums. The Colonel has been talking about closing the areas before something serious happens."

Behind us the diner's proprietor had finally broken the stalemate over corn by telling the anglers to try Velveeta cheese.

The goal of all modern administrators—whether they work for the government or an industry—is to serve the greatest number of people with the best facsimile of whatever experience they are seeking in the shortest possible time. This is true whether the people are touring a National Park or Disney World, eating dinner at a fast-food restaurant or aboard a cruise ship, or fishing and hunting. Proportionately, for every additional person the administrators process through the check-in and check-out lines, the value and meaning of whatever experience is being sought diminishes for everyone.

We often seem so obsessed with counting and measuring things that we have really come to believe the only value of anything, including life itself, is numbers. We say a man is *successful* only if we mean he has made a lot of money and we can measure his "worth" in dollars and cents.

State fish and game agencies, and certain nongovernmental conservation groups, too often sustain this numerical view of the outdoors by following political paths of least resistance. Statistics are generated to show that an undersirable situation is at least tolerable and certainly better than risking security to fight for what is right.

Of course, one problem is defining what is right. If a waterfowl manager is more concerned with "maximizing" (a quaint term, perhaps first used in industrial accounting) "shooter opportunities" than in preserving natural diversity, he naturally feels his first responsibility is to pump more mallards into the pipeline rather than to help restore beleaguered species like the canvasback or black duck.

Since 1978, when federal biologists first recommended that states within the Atlantic Flyway adopt "a position opposing the continued release of game-farm mallards to the wild," a controversy has raged among state biologists as to whether their primary responsibility is to the shooter, whose license fee pays their bills, or to the resources, including black ducks, they are pledged to protect. (One important cause of the black duck's decline is the swamping of the species' genetic gene pool by pen-raised mallards.)

Some states within the black duck's traditional nesting range have accepted the federal recommendation, but not on the biological or aesthetic grounds on which it was proposed. Maine, for example, terminated its mallard release program simply because it wasn't working. The six-week-old ducklings put into roadside ponds and ditches were easy pickings for a host of predators ranging from snapping turtles to bald eagles, and most of the relatively few survivors flew out of the area before opening day and were collected by shooters elsewhere in New England or further south.

Once the Pennsylvania Game Commission boasted of how far away state-bred mallards were being recovered (e.g., Alaska, Newfoundland, and Jamaica, B.W.I.), but complaints from hunting-license buyers within the state about all the dollars that were flying elsewhere encouraged the Commission to adopt a lower profile on this program until it was stopped last year.

That part of me which enjoys shooting will miss the Pennsylvania program, but few of us are exclusively shooters; we are also hunters, which means we are or should be imbued with a conservationist's concern about the resources we harvest.

Speaking as a hunter, I recognize that the wily black duck offers superior sport to pen-raised mallards. And speaking as a conservationist, I know wild black ducks are better able to prevail on any wintering and nesting grounds they may share with feral mallards. In the winter, black ducks know how to exploit coastal marshes that rarely freeze, while pen-raised mallards depend on the handouts of suburbanites or starve. In the spring a parasite, leucocytzoan—whose intermediate host is the black-fly prevalent throughout eastern Canada and New England—devastates mallard broods but has little impact on black ducks. In fact, this parasite may constitute one of the reasons black ducks evolved as a distinct species in eastern North America four million or so years ago—about the same time our own ancestors were getting started in Africa and Asia.

However, some mid-Atlantic biologists could care less about the history, aesthetics, or even biology of the matter. All they know is that black ducks have been steadily declining for two decades—mostly, according to retired federal waterfowl biologist Walter F. Crissey, due to overshooting—while mallards have suddenly escalated in abundance—mostly from Maryland's duck stamp program, which annually turns every penny above administrative costs to the rearing and release of tens of thousands of mallards—more birds in a year than Maine and Pennsylvania biologists ever dreamed of producing!

Seeing Pennsylvania comply with the federal request to stop releasing game-farm birds, and perhaps nervous that even Maryland would reconsider its short-term-pleasures program; *Virginia Wildlife,* that commonwealth's conservation magazine, published an article this past spring ridiculing the federal position opposing pen-raised mallard releases. A good many Maryland mallards are shot each year in Virginia, and doubtless that state's Commission of Game and Inland Fisheries doesn't want to lose this free lunch.

The *Virginia Wildlife* article was subtle in its distortion of the facts. First, it pointed out that mallards have always existed in the Atlantic Flyway—of course they have, but not game-farm birds possibly carrying a variety of domestic poultry diseases, which can be spread to wild birds; and that mallards and black ducks are taxonomically the same species—even though in some significant respects they differ behaviorally as well as being distinguished by blood type, which makes the mallard susceptible to the leucocytzoan and the black duck far less so.

The article went on to say that the mallard has increased and the black duck decreased due to changes in coastal wintering habitat. The article did not explain why, after a decade of coastal marsh and estuary protection, the black duck continues its slide toward oblivion. Nor did it dwell much on the influence of 70,000 to 100,000 mallards per year being dumped into prime mid-Atlantic winter habitat for black ducks where a significant proportion of all the black ducks we have left will be choosing partners for the following spring's reproduction.

My favorite lines from this state-endorsed piece went like this: ". . . the decline of the black duck is no real decline at all. It means the success of the mallard is not the case of one species replacing another, like one nation overwhelming another by storm. Far from that. What it boils down to is a replacement of one color phase of mallard by another color phase of mallard. And what's wrong with that?"

If such reasoning sounds plausible to you, you clearly value shooting over hunting. And if you don't understand the difference between these two activities, I can only recommend you take one of the better state hunter education courses, like those offered by Minnesota or Missouri. Such remedial reading in conservation would also be useful for an unfortunately large number of waterfowl biologists in all four flyways.

Some state fishery managers are as caught up in "maximizing opportunity" as many of their wildlife counterparts. Awarding "certificates of achievement" to people for killing large fish seems more prevalent among state conservation agencies than education concerning the aesthetic values of fish and fishing, or the biological value of saving native fishes with funny names like sucker, chub, and darter.

If a monster catch was an overage female that had already done queen-ant duty in the state hatchery before being dumped into the lake or river where it was recaught by an elated angler, the "certificate of achievement" is only a surreal adjunct to a surreal fishery.

But when a species is troubled and stocks cannot easily be made up with hatchery products, the competition between states to see which can lay claim to the biggest of the beleaguered caught within their borders is grotesque.

Currently, the bluefin tuna and Atlantic coastal striped bass are such threatened species. Both fishes show all the characteristics of a resource nearing exploitive extinction.

First, the average size of these fishes has increased dramatically. In the case of the tuna, the definition of what constitutes a giant rose from 300 pounds in the 1950's to 700 pounds today. In the case of the striper, a huge cow bass once weighed 50 pounds; in the past couple of years, the 70-pound mark has been broken several times by both commercial and recreational fishermen—although along the Atlantic coast the distinction between these two activities is not always clear.

A trophy-sized tuna or striper caught on rod and reel is as

likely to be sold to a restaurant as it is to be taken home and eaten by the friends and family of the angler. In either case, all trophies are too "valuable" to be released.

Any striped bass over 35 pounds is a female, twelve or thirteen years of age, and capable of laying nearly 5,000,000 eggs. Her smaller, four-year-old sister, just beginning to spawn, can produce no more than 65,000 eggs. Obviously, for the sake of the resource, the younger fish is more expendable than the older "cow." However, all too many fishermen, particularly those motivated and reinforced by fishing contests, including many sponsored by state fish and game agencies, are more likely to release the small striped bass or tuna—"to give them a chance to grow up"—than the larger, more fertile fish. That is, if they release anything at all.

Resource managers are handicapped by antique notions of success that say "the bigger the better" and in the case of troubled species—be they black ducks or bluefins—the managers can no longer suggest meaningful regulations, even if administrators or legislatures would be willing to listen.

Working with year-old data on threatened species is about as useful as working with nineteenth-century information. Expected catches or quotas for both striped bass and bluefin tuna have gone unfulfilled for the past several years despite increasing fishing pressure as each species' price has gone up.

Yet, in the meantime, fishing contests along the coast from Maine to the Carolinas are still eager to have the biggest, deadest striped bass or tuna on the docks alongside the lucky angler so his or her picture can be sent to newspapers "proving" that the good life exists wherever this particular bass or tuna happened to end its life.

Competition is presently most ferocious between the professional boosters of New York, New Jersey, and Massachusetts, where all the very largest tuna and stripers are being taken.

Of course, it is preposterous to say that a striped bass,

perhaps born in the Potomac River between Maryland and Virginia, which has wintered in North Carolina and summered in Cape Cod Bay, should be termed a "New York striper" or a "Massachusetts bass."

The coast is one ecological package. If stripers do not find good spawning conditions in the Chesapeake, good wintering conditions in North Carolina, *and* good foraging in New Jersey, New York, and New England, there will be no more coastal striped bass fishery.

Yet rather than admit such a thing—which means admitting that we need a reciprocal recreational saltwater fishing license among all the Atlantic states to protect our many far-wandering game-fishes—many sportsmen beat their chest about the sea being the last frontier, while our more pious brethren tell us not to worry: that God will look after the stripers, the tuna, and us.

Under such circumstances, catch-and-kill fishing competitions become analogous to foresters searching the woods for champion trees, then cutting them down and bringing them in to prove that they once existed.

Thus, I am pessimistic, not only because I believe the quality of our hunting and fishing will continue to deteriorate in its diversity of species and variety of experiences, but because it appears that most hunters and fishermen will accept these declines as inevitable, like fate. They will be glad they got theirs when they did, but they will be disappointed their children don't always believe their stories of how good things used to be.

I am not a cynic, though. I retain the illusion that as outdoorsmen we do not have to settle for second- and third-rate experiences. As conservationists, we may be fighting rear-guard actions against the overwhelming momentum of the people-processors and the numbers players. But, the fight is right and just, and that in itself offers a first-rate experience. Like Lincoln, I'd just as soon wrestle with the muddy pig as wonder what happened to it. §

# Always Richard

*Art Lee*

THE FADING LIGHT is behind the canoe, a bank of pink cementing the sky to the valley walls. The moon is rising. The night will be clear and cool. Already stars have begun to show, and the river looks black and secretive, all definition lost with the diminishing light. The guide sits staring astern, his elbow resting on a gunwale. The canoe is steady, and you wonder whether salmon are moving up in the darkness under you. One fish lies in a bed of ferns in the bow, and you are ready to concede the other that would fill out your limit. You are ready to quit.

"One more drop," Richard declares without discussion. He pulls the killock, and the canoe, kept in line with a paddle Richard uses as a rudder, drifts along sixty feet toward the tail of the pool. Slowly, he lets the anchor rope slide through his free hand, and there is a subtle jolt as the canoe, pushed by the current, reaches the end of it. Richard tracks the shore through narrowed eyes to verify he is exactly where he wants to be and nods. "Okay," he says finally with the authority of a ship's captain, and you begin to fish another drop.

"Should I change flies, you think?" you ask.

"What do you have on . . . Black Dose? Ah, the very best. A salmon's not forgetful like an old bachelor." Richard's brogue drifts back from under the wide brim of a Borsalino hat as it has all day with stories of old Indian guides, logging camps, pretty women, good liquor and salmon, mostly salmon. The memories are meticulous and seem to tumble over you like the waterfall of white hair that tumbles over his shirt collar. When Richard tells a story or gives advice, you listen, because there is only one Richard Nelson Adams. He is the best at what he does, and though he'd never say so, he knows it, too.

Richard Adams is dean of Atlantic salmon fishing guides on Québec's Matapédia River on the Gaspé Peninsula. He personifies the unaffected man in an unaffected setting, master of river and forest, so famous thereabouts that he has been sought out by Canadian television for interviews, is guest of and companion to millionaires, and, occasionally, even signs an autograph. His letters are cherished by those who receive them, including corporation presidents. Each one is signed, "Always, Richard," which his sports will tell you, *says it all.*

"God didn't make too many Adamses like Richard," he informs you with his disarming way of talking about himself in the third person. "People ask me if this Adams or that Adams is related to Richard. I tell 'em, 'If he's a nice fella, he is. If he's not, he's not.' " To be related to Richard Adams and to have him acknowledge it is an important matter in the Matapédia River valley.

Character-actor handsome, Richard is aging, but he still runs better than he walks and walks better than he sits. He handles a twenty-seven-foot Gaspé canoe in heavy current as if it's trained, and he'd rather fish for salmon than do anything else in the world. The river, the fish and the sportsmen he guides are, in fact, his world. Richard guides each day of a ninety-day season as though it could be his last, often keeping his sport at it long after all the other boats are in. He's been doing it that way since he was twelve years old.

"Look here." Richard likes to talk flat out. "I'd be ashamed if I didn't respect the salmon. Listen . . . Some friends of mine told me years ago, 'Richard, we feel sorry for you working every Sunday.' And I said 'What the hell do you want to be feeling sorry for me for? I might go to church, but after that what am I going to do?' " His meaning is clear. He'd be fishing salmon.

Richard flourishes at the center of attention, and like most celebrities, he is an instinctive showman. To think he isn't jealous of his reputation would be naive, but to believe his image is contrived would be to misunderstand the man and the essential nature of his profession. Richard's reputation is based on a lifetime of hard work and accumulated knowledge. His reputation is the foundation of his image, and, like that of any gifted sports or entertainment personality, is perpetuated not so much by the man himself as by those people he plays to. To Richard it's simple. "I try to please everybody the best I know how," he says, "and, I try never to dress better than my sport."

A hundred miles from home, Richard could roam the streets and nobody would recognize him. But he's the kind of man who would always be noticed. His face might have been chiseled from driftwood, and behind deep-set, blue eyes lie thousands of salmon, either killed or lost, each one etched on his memory as if it were hooked only yesterday. Richard wears flannel shirts, suspenders he calls braces, an old cashmere sweater with a hole in the right elbow, a thick leather belt with a big brass buckle and Mountie breeches, laced tightly at the calf. Always, day or night, his wide-brimmed hat he is fond of saying would set you back two hundred dollars if you went out to buy it today is not far away. Richard Adams looks more like a guide than anyone has a right to.

"I came up to the Matapédia on the drive that spring of the year, forty years ago," he says, "Chrissalmighty, I was just a colt, young and good looking." Richard is holding court before a group of sports and their guides as he does every afternoon between beats on the river. The July sun is high, and there's no sense in fishing. Richard is standing while the others sit, a measure of his status.

"The manager told me to check the Causapscal River, thirty-two miles up. Well, sir, I went up on snowshoes, and when I came back, he asks me, 'Richard, how long will it take to bring the logs down from Big Brook?' And I told him with a hundred and forty men to put the river in shape, we could be in in five or six days." Richard pauses and stares into his tumbler of rum, ice and whatever mixer happens to be handy when someone is pouring. The best previous time, he reports, had been about two weeks. "We brought her in in five and a half days."

Richard is able somehow to haunt old times—days when just six boats fished almost seventy miles of river—without seeming to lord it over those who missed them. Although he had guided the lower reaches of the Matapédia and on the Restigouche when he was a boy, he was first introduced to the upriver beats he loves best in 1939 by R. J. Cullan, then president of the International Paper Company. Until the late 1960's, "the company," as Richard always calls it, operated several fishing camps to entertain important clients and other guests.

"Well sir," clucks the guide, "the old man, Mr. Cullan himself, asked me to come up for two weeks to help put things in order. He said the guides he had didn't even know where to set the seats in a canoe. Boys, I got thirty-five years out of it."

Richard quickly became Cullan's personal guide and confidant, and when Cullan "went to Heaven, like all salmon fishermen and pretty girls," Richard was inherited by his successor, John Hinman. The company's river holdings on the Matapédia and Causapscal rivers were bought up by Québec Province, which has managed them since 1969 by sector for unlimited public access or through a system of limited bookings. Richard now guides on the prime stretches, dubbed by anglers "the millionaires' zone."

RICHARD'S IMPRESSIONS OF HIMSELF, his times and life in general are often bold, but he draws on a singular wit to keep things in perspective. "The first time I drank water out of a running tap," he recalls, "was at the Restigouche Salmon Club. I was seven years old, I think. We'd always gotten our water in a wooden bucket and drank it from a dipper . . . the tap water didn't hurt me too much, though.

"Me, I have to say I must have made a mistake. I fell in love with horses before women . . . I changed my mind later. . . . But, maybe I did the right thing, aye? If you spend a lot of time with the salmon and the bears, you can't always smell sweet."

In an area where cultural differences at times trouble both English and French residents, Richard seems to emerge as everybody's favorite, although he doesn't appear to play at politics. He speaks fluent French and often rams back and forth recklessly from one language to the other. He is also the valley's most colorful historian. "Lord Mount Stephen he came to the valley a hundred years ago to push the railroad through," as Richard tells it. "And, by God, when he found the salmon, and the pretty French girls started washing his back with good lye soap, well, he wouldn't even go back to sign the checks in Québec City where he was supposed to be holding the reins."

Richard portrays the days when he took to the woods with the logging crews in the middle of October and didn't come out until the middle of May. He knows how to build a skow to hold fifty men, milk cows, and make equipment by fashioning elbows from roots and trunks of spruce to hold the planks to the keel. He recalls eating salted pork and beef every day, marble cake, molasses and butter once a week, and he still refers to all food as grub. He can also remember working for fifty cents a day "and glad I was, by God, to get it. Hell, I was working, and what more could a man ask for, for sure?"

Richard considers himself a lucky man and thanks changes in salmon fishing for it. "Do you think the sport would take an old guide into the hotel and give him a couple of glasses of gin in those days?" he asks. "Well, I'd say not . . . No use to talking. We had a little lunch and boiled the kettle alongside the river. Me, I was forty years old before I got my first drink of hard liquor. But, I'm getting used to it.

"Do I love the salmon? Chrissalmighty, I guess I do. I owe the salmon everything. Do you think I'd be standing here right now with the likes of all of you—with so many friends and stories to remember—if it wasn't for the salmon? Why, I'da probably been at home with an old wife to tell everybody, *Le pauvre chien est fatiqué,* the poor dog is tired."

RICHARD TAKES A LIBERAL GULP of rum and leads a procession down the bank to the stoop of his little cabin, set in a grove of spruce that overlooks the river. The cabin is painted the traditional white and green of a salmon camp, and although it has no running water or electricity, he prefers it to a handsome home he owns in the town of Matapédia, about twenty miles downriver. Richard always arrives ahead of the others by enough strides to offer everyone a place to sit. He is especially attentive to the ladies.

"It's the reel that counts," he declares. "With a good reel with a proper brake, you're good for three generations. A sport I was guiding a couple of years back he hooked a big fish, well over twenty pounds, and tried to play it off one of those cheap, single-action reels. Some tourists came down from the highway road and wanted to take a picture. It was about four o'clock, and the sun was down in that sport's good-lookin' face. One of the people asked me in French, "When do you expect to get the fish?' I looked over at the sport. He was having a bad time of it. 'We expect to get it tonight,' I told them.

"When we finally got the fish, I asked the sport, 'Will you do Richard a favor?' He said, 'Sure,' and I said, 'Will you take off that reel, for Godalmighty sake, and give it to some schoolboy to fish trout?' You know, he did just that and the next season didn't he come back with one fit for fighting fish."

If it's possible for Richard to become impatient, it's with the playing of salmon. He likes heavy tackle for the big fish of the Matapédia River and favors the old feather-winged fly patterns—the Green Highlander, Black Dose, Silver Doctor and Dusty Miller—in double hooks and large sizes to the newer and, some argue, more effective hairwing dressings. If Richard had his way, no one would be allowed on the river, even in low water, with a leader tippet lighter than twelve-pound test. "If you gave me my choice of pools right today," he declares, "and I had only this one day to fish, I'd be using nothing but good old twenty-five-pound test. Yessir. Any fish that'll run into a net on the open sea, you think he's afraid of a leader? Well, I guess he's not."

Richard pushes you to play your salmon hard, to bull them, and anglers he feels are pussyfooting can spark some of his saltiest remarks. A sport who suddenly found his fish running upriver after being played timidly for almost an hour asked, "Do you think I should follow him, Richard?"

"Why not," snapped the guide. "You'll be a hundred feet farther from the Bay of Chaleur."

There is a pool on the Matapédia named for him, Richard tells sportsmen and guides alike, although, of course, the guides already know it well. It may, in fact, be the best pool on the river and is certainly the best to be fished by wading.

"We didn't fish it very often," Richard remembers. "The pool was on the lower end of our water, and we had so much water upstream. When we did fish it, we had never seen a fish. To tell the truth, I was going to call it Black Duck Pool." He pauses and shakes his head meaningfully. "Anyway, I was guiding this pretty woman one day, and she told me she'd like to fish it," he continues. " 'It's such a beauty. Does it have a name?' she asked me. I told her, 'No, it doesn't. We haven't baptized it yet.' And she said, 'Richard, if we get a salmon out of it today, I'll see to it that we call it Richard's Pool.' Well, I told her she had a deal, and didn't we hook a lively salmon on a Silver Doctor, and I carried her across the pool on my back to get it. Good as her word, she went back to the Old Man, and he decided to call the pool for Richard. Why, if a man never had any more water than that one pool, he'd have plenty of water for a lifetime."

RICHARD GLANCES at the sky. The sun is low, and he knows it's almost time to fish again. Before they go back to their beats, he thanks everyone for visiting with him, occasionally apologizes for doing most of the talking, and offers around a dipper of spring water.

As you fish, even when you are cold and ready to quit, you

can't help but admire this man who is guiding you. There is a special elegance about a man who knows good food but has drunk so much muddy water in his lifetime. You have watched him as he waves to passing trains. He has ridden them to Campbelton, New Brunswick, he tells you, and to Québec City and Montreal. He says he would like to ride one all the way to Mexico City without even explaining why, but as you come to know him better, you have to wonder if Richard Nelson Adams doesn't truly believe that every train in the Western Hemisphere eventually stops in Matapédia.

"We were in this after-hours place in Montreal, this young friend and me." Richard makes the canoe fast to a makeshift dock on the rim of the pool you'd been fishing. The last rays of light are gone, and his face is silhouetted in moonlight. "And this little girl, not wearing very much harness, comes up to me.

" 'I'll spend the whole night with you,' she says, 'if you have some money.' Now, I ask her, 'How much might that be costing?' just to be polite, you know.

" 'Twenty-five dollars,' she says, looking me right square in the eye.

" 'Twenty-five dollars?' I said to her. 'Godalmighty, girl, that's the daily rate for a tractor.' " §

# James Dean Quail

*Thomas McIntyre*

I HAVEN'T HUNTED QUAIL nearly as much as I'd like. California, where I live, is perfectly fine quail country, but I could easily number on the fingers of my two hands every quail hunt I was ever on. Part of this comes from my not owning any dogs and feeling dumb about trying to hunt quail without them, but the bigger part comes from my flat missing a good bet.

I remember my first quail hunt. How at age 11 or 12 I rode in a station wagon into the Western Sierra foothills after a winter rain. The country was as achingly green as only the semiarid California landscape can become immediately after a heavy rain—the land soaking up the water and swelling into a verdant sponge—and the dirt road had turned to slick, wet clay. We turned in on a crowned drive dropping down into a muddy ranch yard, and there below and off to the side of the drive was a ranch pickup lying on its roof like a dying tortoise. The old bandy-legged rancher came out to greet us, a soiled Stetson tipped low over his eyes. In the early-morning light he looked vague and bleary and explained that for some reason he had had minor difficulty negotiating the road back home the night before. Could we help him right his truck?

I cannot recall whether we did, or whether another truck was on hand, but I do recall riding in the back of *a* pickup, feeling cold and cranky while a wet Irish setter with the worst case of mange I had ever seen clopped excitedly all over my legs. Of the hunt itself I can recall the 20 gauge being too long and the empty gamebag slapping against the back of my legs as I glumly trudged over most of the state of California; how the quail would flush far in front of me and sail uphill under the gray sky while everybody's shotgun but mine went *bang;* how I just gawked wide-eyed. I was brought back to that ranch some months later to be shown firsthand what cowboys did to calves at roundup time, and after that I wasn't real sure how genuinely cut out I was for a life in the West.

Other quail hunts followed, primarily search-and-destroy missions with a bunch of the guys from high school to an abandoned mine site in the Mojave Desert where we would desultorily shoot rabbits and chukar and quail during the day, then char them black over a raging campfire at night, washing down their partially cooked flesh with iced beers we would drink as recklessly as only foolish high-school boys can drink beers they have cajoled some adult into "scoring" for them.

The dawn with a big desert moon growing pale above the western mountains would invariably find us paralyzed, lying on the ground where we had been struck down during the night, trying to puzzle out why we had *ever* wanted to have a time as simply bitchin' as this.

Then there was a glass-clear winter's day many years later when I found myself on a thoroughbred ranch off the Ortega Highway in the hills behind San Juan Capistrano, where the swallows come back every year. Friends had invited me to join them in jump-shooting coots and teal out of a cattle pond; and we did, the rancher giving us exactly ten minutes to deploy ourselves in the tall cover surrounding the pond and to lurk in concealment there until he came barreling over the ridge in his pale-blue '57 Chevy, dust swirling behind him in his vortex and his 350-cubic-inch engine making its throaty rumble, driving right down to the pond's edge and sending the waterfowl off the water and high into the air over us; and after all that I succeeded in killing precisely one green-winged drake. Then, on our way back out to the paved highway, a covey of California valley quail hastened across the ranch road in front of us and we were bailing out of the vehicles, loading our shotguns, chasing these quail into the scrub flats, booming away at them. The entire episode had the flavor of an attempted gangland slaying, and it also made me begin to realize, as I stumbled over the deadfall oaks, the cactus and granite rocks, that I really ought to start dressing in slap-shoes and a rubber nose if I was going to insist upon hunting quail in such a fashion.

In fact, I might never have learned what true quail hunting was supposed to be like if I hadn't finally accepted an invitation to go out of state and hunt bobwhite down in Georgia, in beggar lice and honeysuckle and over-skilled English pointers. Down there the dogs are tall and bony, and when one of them would go on point on a quail, the tail high, the dog's entire spine defining a fluid downward arc like a wave cresting— the dog behind him honoring that point with the mannered courtesy of a Southern gentleman—I began to experience after only a few days of hunting the kind of quail epiphany I'd been groping for during all my years of bozoing around.

I am, however, an unregenerate Westerner; more to the point a *native* Californian like my father and his father before him—everyone before that, as near as I can determine, Irish bumpkins—and when I returned home I felt it was something akin to a duty that I find a respectable hunt like that Georgian one, only with my own wild California quail as the quarry.

It took some looking, but I did find it one October day on a ranch in the central Coast Range. It was north of Paso Robles, east of the Salinas River—the "largest subterranean stream in America"—in the rugged live-oak and digger-pine canyons of those coastal mountains.

Really, there isn't much to tell. The Brittany spaniels found the coveys in the early morning while the dewy ground still held their scent. The little dogs were belled, and when they vanished into the thick chaparral along the dry creekbeds we knew they had a point as soon as the tolling ceased. Then it was the slow but deliberate walk up through the rust-brown buckwheat or the chamise or the yerba santa, the Wingmaster held high, ready for the birds to flush in the way only wild birds will, ready to bring the gun to my shoulder and for my eyes to select and follow a quail in full driving flight.

Other times we found them among the live oaks on the high ridges—an unlikely place. Before I could even get my gun on him, I would see a cock bird become airborne and lay his black topknot against his head and in a visible shift in gears go to after-burners and streak to the bottom of the canyon.

Still other times the flushed birds flew to instant roost in the nearest oak, thick with leaves still dark green and with a heavy crop of acorns bright as new money. I stood under the tree, throwing rocks and deadwood into it, shaking its branches, or staring up and making—what?—"quailwing" noises with my lips. You know, a sort of *prprprprp*-ing to see if I could get the quail to fly out. On that hunt it seemed somehow *perfectly* acceptable to be standing there, producing vulgarities with my lips, because the hunting that day, all things considered, was as respectable as I could have hoped for. At any rate, I was not ashamed, and though I missed a number of birds, a number also died, died as nicely as could be, the dogs gathering them up and delivering them to my hand with barely a feather mussed. Maybe there was something to tell after all.

When I took my California quail home that night to cook and eat them, I knew I had made a discovery of no small significance. At last, in my own home state, I had found a place I could return to again and again to make decent Christian quail hunts, to pursue a game animal as it was meant to be pursued: here was a place where I could do it *right* for a change. It was an honor to know of such country, even with all its ghosts.

Perhaps I should explain that that country is surely haunted. All you have to do is walk far up some dry canyon and, looking down, see seashells beneath your feet to be reminded that what you are walking on was once the bottom of the ocean. You can wonder how many Indians and Conquistadors and Franciscan monks once passed through that country and never know the number. How many farmers died behind their plows; how many ranchers riding after strays? In this country John Steinbeck lived. In it James Dean died.

It was on old Route 466 where it met Route 41 near Cholame just outside Paso Robles. They have a stainless-steel monument there now, with obligatory quotes from André Gide and James Dean's name and the date and time and a little symbol for infinity ($\infty$) after it. He was driving his Porsche Spyder to a race in the town of Salinas a quarter of a century ago, and late on the last day of September a Ford sedan driven by a college student turned in front of him and he crashed into it.

I liked James Dean's moody performances in his movies, liked *Rebel Without a Cause* and the couple of others he was in, wish there were more of them. As I take a bite of quail and spit a No. 8 copper-plated pellet onto the china, I have this dippy idea that if somehow he could have just gotten involved in hunting instead of motor sports, if he'd been coming up to that country to have a respectable quail hunt instead of to burn rubber, then there might have been more James Dean movies today. Or there might not. I take another bite of white meat and suppose that even hunting wild California quail is no guarantee that we won't all turn into ghosts in the end—though it certainly is worth the try. §

53

# Downstream

*Jim Capossela*

JUST DOWNSTREAM there waits a different world of trout fishing. It's only a cast beyond the comfort of routine, an impulse past all the experts and the pools with names. It's a forgotten river, wide and full, where both sides are the bank that no one ever walks.

Here there are languid carp that cruise like taxis in the lee of monolithic boulders. And horn-ribbed bullfrogs, that belch from stagnant pools behind a levee of spring mud. But here too is excitement: The thrill of being alone on strange new water, the feeling, once again, that everything is in its place.

If it was hard for me to break away, to the bigger water, to the unknown, it was doubly hard for my angling friends. One late spring day we were tying flies in the cabin, waiting out a pelting, 4:00 p.m. thunderstorm, when I raised the impossible heresy.

"Why don't we go downstream tonight . . . way downstream. Who knows?"

The response was prompt and incisive.

"There's nothing but chubs down there."

"But there's just too many guys in the no-kill section," I said.

"Yeah, but I *know* we'll catch fish there," came the retort.

I know we'll catch fish there. The statement echoed in my head, blotting out the nailing of the rain on the stovepipe. It was the voice of a powerful force: Security—the external kind. That was what brought us back to the same section—no *pool*—night after night, to elbow like squatters for our precious eight feet of river. Security. We knew every dent of water and every knob of rock—like a memorized jigsaw puzzle. All the hatches, too. *Cornuta* spinners at 6:30. Number 12 dark caddis at 7:00. Then, scattered *Isonychia* duns, sulphurs at 8:20—or was it 8:25? Lastly, sulphur spinners right at dark. Not that the fishing was easy. But if we missed an equation, there'd always be a scientist nearby.

"*Paraleptophlebia mollis,*" a chap once corrected me in a dead, even tone of voice.

Trains. The hatches would come in like trains. In fact the entire experience had become like commuting. The river was a set of train tracks, the banks, platforms, with two rows of crowded men, facing each other—and another day—without enthusiasm.

The light of a low sun filled the cabin as the rain stopped. The silence snapped the trance.

"Well *I'm* going downstream," I blurted, as if the conversation of 20 minutes before had never stopped. "I'd rather catch chubs in solitude than spend one more night in that menagerie."

One of my two companions remained unfazed, but amazingly, the other said, "I'll go with you." I swear my car balked at the crossroads that evening, when I turned right instead of left.

The rewards were immediate. We drove over new country

roads and saw farms with deer-edge fields and hemlock barns. We passed backwoods villages with impossible names and one-dog main streets with nothing astir. The mountains had been washed in the hands of the storm, and the earth seemed fresh and new.

"It's too big—it's just too big!" was my riverside reaction. "Too wide . . . no pools . . . all white water. Can we wade it . . . but what . . ."

The pits of insecurity settled in our stomachs as the great size of the water came into wide-angle focus. We walked out to the ancient steel trestle, where you could see a mile or more upstream. There wasn't a soul in sight.

"A good mechanic," one once told me as he contemplated my engine block, "spends half his time just looking." I found a big rock and sat there for a long time, searching for clues.

That's what I remember most about that first evening downstream: Sitting on that big floodplain, feeling almost close to the ocean; not seeing anyone, not expecting to. There were shimmering poplars that flanked the streambank willows, and Queen Anne's Lace growing among the stones. Black-eyed Susans, too, and countless stonefly cases on the scuttled river rocks. For once, I wasn't worried about anyone stealing my "position" or my trout.

Now and then I could see rise-forms way out in some rare slower water, midstream. I looked around, as if for advice, but there was no textbook to turn to. I clinch-knotted a No. 12 Adams, and stepped into the river.

"Hey—those are some kind of really big fish!" I said out loud.

It was far too long a cast, so I waded out intrepidly. At once the water locked my legs like a giant sumo wrestler. I wasn't a good enough wader to fight this terrific current. I wasn't a good enough caster to get out to the fish. I was back on the floodplain, smiling at the giant river that flowed by like a silent master.

I never did reach those fish—but had my companion? Even as he came through the night fog, his smile was visible.

"Got a 16-inch rainbow! Lost a bigger one, too. But they were right in the middle. You just had to pick a spot where you could get out to them."

"Right—without drowning," I added.

"Anyway," he continued happily, "looks like I won't have to suffer through that 'chub meunière' you were threatening to make. There really are trout down here!"

That proved to be the last trip of the season, and soon after my friend drifted away. Not too surprisingly, I drifted right back to the womb: the no-kill section and the same old pool. It had its attractions. In fact, on most of the better trout streams today, the no-kill sections have the best water quality

and number and size of the fish. What's more, these same sections, with the famous pools named after revered ancients and immortal anglers, are often the prettiest—a big reason they're singled out for special regulations.

For me, though, it was like going back home after college, and it would never be the same again. Early the following season, I grew restless, intolerant of any fishermen within sight of me. I'd spend one day on the no-kill—my shot of security—then two days drifting downstream. I started to act and feel a little like a boy again; wherever the river led me, that was fine.

I'd search maps to find bends where the stream left the road. I'd scan topos to find the steepest sections, the ones most apt to keep others away. As I'd done with private and sacred woodcock covers, I'd name these nameless waters myself. There was the Staircase Pool—never caught a thing there—the Trout Lily Pool, Merganser Run.

High water temperature is the number one bane of the downstream trout angler; a thermometer is essential. "Brookies, high 60s. Rainbows, mid 70s. Browns, high 70s." I memorized the limits, but did not let them limit me. If the water was too warm—and it seldom was, except in the dead of summer—I'd fish anyway. I tied up huge marabou muddlers to con the river smallmouths. I even learned to embrace the lowly chub; a 15-incher that mauled a Black Ghost will long be remembered.

Many theories have been laid down to explain success in trout fishing: use of the right fly, proper presentation, timing. I've always believed it comes from studying and learning an individual river. Downstream was a new river that had to be learned all over again.

Entry 5—Same tan caddis as upstream, but a good week earlier. Trout just as selective.

Entry 11—Good Hendrikson hatch. Same fly size (12).

Entry 25—Fishermen (both bait and fly) in local ginmill all fish after dark. Is *that* the answer to this river?

Entry 33—Incredible fall of Trico spinners at 7:30, but no fish working. Water too deep?

The lessons were many, the solutions few. But the rewards were always there. Sometimes it was the sight of a backwash family of geese; a new wildflower spied along a 100-yard-wide floodplain; even occasionally, large trout.

I was fishing tight against a rocky bank one evening, just below a near-vertical tributary. The air was electric.

It was nearly dark when a terrific fall of spinners hit the water and brought some *very* large dorsal fins to the surface. I identified the fly quickly and correctly—unusual for me—and even had a few in my box. Then it was easy. Three fair-sized fish fell in succession, and finally, a deceivingly gentle sip was followed by a doubled rod as the savage raced for the far bank.

Five minutes later, in the shallow instream channel, I measured the brown against my forearm: He came just to my knuckle joint. I let him slip back, but as I waded once more into casting position, I became aware of a distinct sensation: Coldness! The river proved to be several degrees cooler than the main river. That tumbling tributary was the reason.

Another big fish, a twin to the first, was netted that night, before I headed home, a smile on my face and icy-cold tributaries on the brain.

In the freestone streams of any mountain watershed, there are always feeders that may run 5° F., 10° F. or more cooler than the main river. This disparity is greatest and most significant downstream. Each feeder the map revealed became the subject of an evening's adventure, and the trout in those downriver sections often did concentrate at such confluences. In summer, I also probed continually with my thermometer, trying to find springholes that breathed life into the long, sun-battered pools. But the happiest discovery came one day in late July at the end of a ferocious heat spell.

I was fishing way downstream, where campground bathers

were reveling in the near-80° F. water temperatures. It was just *too* hot, so I decided to make the 20-mile drive to another fork of the river, a fork that emanated from a deep, cold reservoir.

I first saw it as a swath of heavy mist, and my eyes grew wide. There'd be no evening mist in this heat, unless. . . . I scrambled down the bank with my thermometer. It was 48° F.! They had been letting water out from the bottom of the reservoir, instead of off the top as previously. This had turned an erstwhile bathtub into a superb trout river. For the next three days, I caught icy-cold jumping browns.

Actually, this was far from an isolated case. Throughout the country, hundreds of deep, watershed reservoirs now release cold water, making previously warm and troutless downriver sections fishable.

Sitting in the cabin one night, I theorized: If downstream represented aloneness (think of it as all-oneness, a guru once advised), imagine how alone I'd be downstream after dark. So one day I drove to a chosen pool, pledging to fish all night and dreaming pipe dreams of ten-pound browns.

It was a steep section of river where anglers never ventured, and I felt somewhat queasy as I clambered down the rocky bank. There was no moon—I'd planned it that way—and the setting sun quickly cast witch-like shadows across the currents. The first bats appeared at exactly 8:30.

While bats never really spooked me before, this evening they seemed to be everywhere. First, one hit my flyline. Then, one nicked the end of my rod. Still another glanced off nearer the handle.

"Radar—I thought they had *radar!*" I said falteringly.

I could no longer concentrate on fishing. Another bat whizzed by my ear. Another seemed to come in at me as if I were a landing strip. Suddenly, horrors of all horrors, a bat stopped and hovered right in front of me—a foot away, eye to eye—like a vampire about to implant the kiss of death. That was all I could take.

I thrashed at him with my rod, but each time he moved just enough so I'd miss him. Then he disappeared . . . but I still felt his presence. A few empty seconds went by before something made me look down. My blood curdled! The bat had landed on me, and was actually climbing up my waders! I reached back for my net, let out, I think, a primeval scream, and thrashed at the monster with such force that I shattered the wooden frame of the net.

With hair on end, I splashed back to shore, through this incredible hatch of bats, and tore up the bank like a mountain goat. I'd finally gone far enough downstream.

On the bluff overlooking the river, I regained my composure, and half-laughed, half-cried at the panic that caused the destruction of my expensive wooden net. Then I looked downriver, where a half-dome of granite cut the water like a knife. Bats nearly forgotten, I started to wonder: "Hmmm, what's down there, down around that bend. Oh, it's probably too big . . . too wide . . . no pools, all whitewater. Still, though, but. . . ." §

# The Pheasant

*William Childress*

THE FIRST PHEASANT I ever shot was in a field near Pusan, Korea. It was 1952, and I shot its head off with an M2 carbine from 30 yards. It was unsporting, but I was a 19-year-old soldier and I had a use for that pheasant. I felt it was only fair to consider it the spoils of war.

Korea is beautiful in the spring. Its high, grassy hills seem to burn with green fire. The people call it "The Land of the Morning Calm," and that fits it perfectly. On still mornings, pale wisps of fog hold the hills like fingers, and wild flowers make jewels for this setting.

But in winter it's a brutal, gray country. Trees are sparse. Centuries of cutting them down for wood have ruined most of the forests. So it was natural enough that the pheasant would be high-stepping through a field where even the straw had been gleaned for fuel.

I remember wondering how the bird had survived thus far

without cover; but the pheasant is a wily bird that manages to exist through all of Asia.

It was a cold November day when I shot the bird. I had been in Korea two months. I had trained as a Demolitions Specialist, MOS 3533. The army made me a Secret Courier. I traveled between Pyongtaek and Pusan with a sealed leather case, a 45 pistol and a submachinegun. This stubby, all-steel weapon was good mainly for noise. I much preferred the light, accurate 30-caliber carbine I was sometimes issued.

I traveled by train, in a railway car compartment, and was told to shoot anyone who tried to take the satchel. It was all a bit cloak-and-dagger and appealed to the kid in me—even though I had seen other kids with little holes in them, through which their lives had leaked. For all I knew, that dispatch case contained nothing but Hershey bars.

It took weeks of practice before I could hit anything with the 45. Some people can score with the thing, but I'm not one, and I don't like it. I fired expertly with the carbine, though, my eye trained by squirrel hunting along the creekbanks of Oklahoma. "Try for the eye or at least the head," my father always told me. "Your 22 won't tear up so much meat that way."

I was free for a day and two nights after dropping off my dispatches in Pusan. A buddy of mine was headquartered there, and we ran around together during the three months I had the job. Pusan was far from the 38th Parallel, and a lively city. But mostly we ignored its entertainments, preferring to requisition a jeep and drive out into the countryside, two gawking farm boys astonished at being in a strange land.

Cleve, my buddy, was an Okie like me, an awkward stalk of a youth with red hair, green eyes and a gap-toothed, engaging smile.

"Whar yonta go t'day?" he would drawl.

"Let's just drive," I'd reply. "I like visiting the villages, getting out among the people, maybe learning a little history and some of the language."

"Ah cain't make heads ner tails of the language."

"I've learned a little."

"Yeah? Say somethin'."

"*Koom-op-soon-nee-dah,*" I said dutifully.

"What's that mean?"

"I think it means, 'Thank you beautifully.'"

"Wal, then, it oughta git ya by most ennywheres," Cleve would say, smiling his gap-toothed smile and pointing the jeep out of the city.

Villages were clusters of mud-walled square houses with thatched roofs. The people enjoyed our curiosity, and discussed Cleve's flaming hair, which amazed them. By signs we made them understand that we, too, were farmers, as all of them were, and this brought approving nods and delighted murmurs. We pantomimed creekbank fishing, and they excitedly pointed toward a river, curving across the valley floor some distance away. We learned they had fished it to extinction, trying to feed themselves.

Like all wartime villages, this was a hungry one, though better off than those nearer the front. In Korea, at 19, I learned how terribly important food is—that in some ways its lack can result in murderous wars. What we took for granted at home, these people struggled for daily. I've never forgotten their hungry faces as they spoke of their river, which once teemed with fish.

Hunting wasn't much better. In the mountains to the north, they said, there were a few deer. But they might have meant cows, and we wouldn't have known it. There were a few birds. . . .

Birds?

Elaborate gestures. Some kind of large, collared bird.

"Cleve," I said, "I think there's ring-neck pheasants around here. Just like those rascals that camp in the grainfields back home. What I wouldn't give for my mutt and a shotgun."

A few miles from the village was a solitary farmhouse. A woman about 35 was beating clothes on a rock. Two small children helped by bringing water. It was obvious she had no soap, and when she saw us she quickly stood and gathered the children to her. The kids wore the badges of malnutrition—thin bodies and pouched-out bellies. We knew what had happened. The ROK army had drafted the husband, leaving the wife and kids to try to keep the tiny farm going.

We drove on, along the floor of a wide valley rimmed by mountains. As we sped past other villages, I had the eerie feel-

ing I was home. The dirt road was as red as any in Oklahoma. Spindly telephone poles lined it. The fields were laid out in neat squares, and there were no fences.

"Hold 'er, Will," Cleve cautioned, and I stopped the jeep. "See 'im? Cuttin' acrost the field like a jackrabbit on skates."

The pheasant looked just like those back home. Here, 10,000 miles from those amber fields, he had brought home to us. I unlimbered the M2.

"I'm gonna take him."

Cleve was skeptical. "Even if you hit him, that slug will make sausage outta him."

"Not if I hit him in the head."

I leveled the carbine. The thick front side obscured the bird, now walking sedately 30 yards away since we did not come closer.

*Whack!*

The carbine bucked and my first shot kicked dirt in front of the bird. He craned his neck, but stayed put. The second round was short, but splashed more dirt, and the bird squawked and leaped sideways. The third shot decapitated him and he kicked a few times in the furrow and died.

Back in the farmyard, the woman and two kids were still at their task. I walked over and handed her the pheasant, its brilliant plumage ruffling in the cold wind. Tears pearled in her eyes as she took it.

"*Koom-op-soon-ne-dah,*" she whispered.

"Happy Thanksgiving," I said, getting back in the jeep and pointing its nose toward Pusan. §

# Pardonable Sins

*Lionel Atwill*

O F ALL THE GAMES I know, none save hunting and fishing permits the players to make up the rules. Now I don't mean the written laws—limits, seasons, and the like—I mean the unwritten handicaps we impose on ourselves in the name of sportsmanship: rules of etiquette, rules of dress, rules of tackle, loads and techniques, rules that we individually are honor-bound to uphold:

"I'd never shoot at a deer over 50 yards."

"Can't see using anything but flies for trout."

"No way would I hunt squirrels with a shotgun. Only a 22 for me."

You know, *those* rules. What I particularly like about them is that no matter how hard we try, we are going to break a few. But such sins are pardonable; and, surprisingly, a temporary fall from grace often brings us closer to the righteous course of good sportsmanship to which we all aspire. Consider:

Weasel Eyes McLaughlin, my college roommate, grew up

in a tiny New York suburb in a house where fine guns were part of the decor, and shooting was an acceptable subject for discussion by men after dinner over brandy and cigars. As a boy, Weasel Eyes learned to shoot trap and skeet with skill. Several times he went South with his father to hunt plantation quail, and in the fall Weasel frequented a nearby pheasant farm.

Weasel Eyes thought of himself as quite the hunter, for sure, but in truth he had never hunted hard and wild in his life.

After college Weasel Eyes went into banking. Despite his nickname, which was less descriptive of his looks than of his personality—you couldn't turn your back on the Weasel for fear he would pour Sal Hepatica in your beer or squire off your girl with promises of screen tests in the south of France—the Weasel did well: vice-presidency in a large New York bank, charming family, lovely house in the suburbs. But hunting somehow slipped by the boards.

Then the Weasel arrived at my house one fall day, the first time we had seen each other in ten years, with a beautiful double and great intentions of controlling what I had described to him as my "plague of grouse."

"Weasel," I told him over breakfast before our first day afield, "these birds aren't easy, you know. They're not those Chinese chickens you used to shoot."

The Weasel flashed his most sardonic grin. No grouse would make a fool of him. "Don't think there will be a problem," he said, then turned to my wife and asked her if she would be interested in a little film project at Saint Tropez.

Two days later the Weasel was singing a different tune. We had caught the birds in that late-fall time when they covey up to gorge and sun and perhaps tell tales of inept hunters before winter settles in. As soon as we stepped into the covert, grouse flew—in singles, doubles and squadrons—and the Weasel started shooting with the fervor of a ten-year-old at a carnival gallery.

I took three birds that first day, and limited out with four the second. The Weasel punched air. He fired a box and a half of shells, trimmed countless spruce, pruned half a dozen apples, and blew apart blackberries, wild roses and barberries at every step. He never touched a grouse.

Over breakfast on the third day the Weasel could not muster up enough spirit to put salt in my coffee or leer at my wife.

"Let's play tennis," he said.

"Weasel, birds, remember. Grouse."

"How about bridge? I'll spot you 500 points."

"Grouse. You can't give up, Weasel. That's not you."

"I'll race you to see who can finish the paper first."

"Grouse, Weasel, grouse."

Reluctantly, he gave in.

We went to an old orchard, overgrown with brambles and edged with spruce, a covert I knew held birds. The Weasel moped. He carried his gun around his knees. His eyes focused on his feet. When we reached the edge, we stopped for a moment, and I heard a soft peeping in the spruce to our left. Cautiously I knelt, peered into the tangle of lower limbs, and saw a fat grouse, neck stretched out, crest raised, head flicking right and left.

"Weasel," I said, "there's your bird."

"Huh," said the Weasel.

"Come over here, very slowly. There's a grouse under that spruce. See him?"

The Weasel looked, saw the birds, and slowly I thought I could see his spirit return. "Take him, Weasel," I said. And he did.

I've heard the Weasel tell the story of that shot a dozen times now, and with each account the bird gets farther off the ground. In truth, of course, the Weasel grounded that grouse, swatted him on the deck with a full charge of 8s. I'm glad he did, even though grouse grounding, in my book, is a heinous sin.

Grounding that grouse made a hunter out of the Weasel. Had he passed up the bird or missed it on the wing, he would have gone home in a foul mood, foreclosed on a few mortgages, raised interest rates a point or two, and then let the weekend slip from his memory. The hunt would have been something to chuckle off. You've heard people do it: "Sure, I went hunting once; couldn't hit a thing, ha, ha, ha . . ."; that condescending laugh as if incompetence afield were a virtue.

When he swatted that bird, though, the Weasel, who truly is an honorable man, made an unspoken pact with me, with the grouse, and with himself to come back and hunt hard and do it right—on the wing. Which, of course, he did.

KISSING FISH is another example. Peter, my best angling buddy, and I went to Labrador last year to fish for big brook trout, six-, seven-, and eight-pound brookies thick as your leg and colorful as a Mardi Gras parade. There are a lot of big fish up in those lakes and rivers, but not so many that a dozen greedy fishermen couldn't clean them out in short order, so the rule of camp was simple: one fish per man—no more.

Pete and I fished hard for five days. We took fish, good fish up to eight pounds, but we could not bring ourselves to kill one; they were too magnificent to die. But on the last day of our stay when everyone in our party had a trophy to take home save the two of us, Pete said, "It's time."

We fished a flowage that afternoon, a short river strewn with glacial boulders that connected two lakes. Pete tied on a streamer and waded into the thigh-deep water beneath a gentle falls. I watched from shore. Pete worked out some line, cast, and immediately a fish hit.

It was a long fight, a battle against current, against a six-pound brookie, against nerves and the ever-present thought of failure. I coached Pete from the bank, not because he needed coaching but because I wanted to share in the fight. I wanted Pete's trophy to have a part of me in it, too.

When the fish finally tired, I jumped in the water to land it, for the guide—and the net—were on the far shore. Clumsily, I grabbed the brookie, lifted it from the water, and cradled it in my arms like a child.

"You want this one, Pete?" I asked.

Pete stammered, tripped, fell to his knees in the stream, got up again, and finally blurted out, "I want him. I want him. That's my fish."

We killed the brookie. He was a beauty, too, with a great kype to his jaw, a crimson sash down his flank, and a semicircular notch in his tail, bitten out by some arrogant, young brookie trying to move up in station in that hostile Labrador world.

After we killed him, we committed one of those pardonable sins: We put on a performance that gave new meaning to the words "uncouth," "ill-mannered" and "undignified." Surely Isaac Walton and friends were rolling in their graves.

We kissed the fish. We passed him back and forth, hugging him and kissing him until our faces were covered with blood and slime; then we ran up and down the bank with the fish held high like a banner, shouting like children until we grew hoarse and the poor fish grew stiff and his colors started to fade.

It was then, I think, that we cried a bit, too.

Fools we were, absolute embarrassing fools, devoid of any trace of the decorum that good fishermen try to maintain. We will remember that fish, though, that beautiful brookie, for a long time.

Grounding grouse, kissing fish, and a thousand other unwritten rules are, I suppose, the factors that make hunting and fishing noble sports. Certainly they are the elements that people who do not hunt or fish will never understand. §

# Daniel Webster and the Great Brook Trout

*Kenneth Shewmaker*

THE STORY SEEMS too good to be true. In 1823, Philip Hone (1780-1851; businessman, diarist, and mayor of New York City from 1825 to 1827) saw an enormous brook trout in the Carmans River just below the tavern owned and operated by Samuel Carman. The Carmans River is on Long Island, and the alleged sighting took place near the town of Brookhaven, which was called the Fire Place in the 1820s. Hone shared his sercet with Daniel Webster (1782-1852; elected United States Senator from Massachusetts in 1827), and the two friends spent several hours unsuccessfully trying to tempt the huge trout into taking a fly. Webster, who was an avid fisherman, became obsessed with the Carmans River leviathan, and four years later he had a second chance.

In 1827, the story continues, the huge brook trout was dislodged from its hiding place because of the repair of a water wheel. It darted from the millrace into the millpond, and soon became the subject of animated conversation at Samuel Carman's tavern. As luck would have it, Webster and Hone, in the company of Martin Van Buren (1782-1862; a United States Senator from New York in 1827), were in town for another fishing excursion that spring. Webster and Hone fished all day Saturday without locating the great trout, and that evening they commiserated by imbibing too much rum at Samuel Carman's inn. Despite their hangovers, or perhaps because of them, Webster and Hone dutifully attended the services at Parson Ezra King's Presbyterian church the next morning. Leaving nothing to chance, however, Carman had stationed his servant (who has been identified as a man named either Apaius Enos or Lige) at the millpond with orders to keep a ready eye out for the big fish. The prophetic hymn of the day, of course, was "Shall we gather at the river, the beautiful, beautiful river."

As the long-winded Parson King droned on, Carman's servant tiptoed into the church with the news that the big brook trout was swimming about in the millpond. Webster, Hone, Carman, and the servant left their pews as inconspicuously as possible. Guessing what was afoot, other members of the congregation also began to slip out, until only the most pious remained. Finally, Parson King, who also was a dedicated fly fisherman, uttered a hasty benediction and headed for the door. The entire congregation gathered at the river to watch the ensuing battle between a great man and a great fish.

Webster first caught a small brookie, which he gently released unharmed. About half an hour later, however, the big fish was hooked. The cast was long, the fly landed daintily, the strike was ferocious, the battle was nearly as protracted as Reverend King's sermon, and the memorable words were uttered by Carman's servant: "We hab you now, sar!" What they allegedly had was a world record-breaking 14½ pound leviathan.

Samuel Carman, the story continues, traced the outline of the great fish against a wall, and Philip Hone transferred Carman's scratches onto a linen. Sometime later, a local blacksmith or carpenter made a wooden replica of the gigantic brook trout. This facsimile served as the weathervane on Parson King's church for fifty years. Unfortunately, the cherrywood plank, which had been made a third larger than the original outline in order to provide it with the proper proportions for the church spire, was struck by lightning, which may explain the splintered appearance of that artifact, which still is in existence.

As for Webster, Hone, and Van Buren, they immediately set out for New York City with their trophy. The trout, which was prepared in a tasty and rich sour cream sauce, was served with white wine at Delmonico's. Daniel Webster, the story concludes, was so delighted with his experience that he sent Samuel Carman one hundred dollars.[1]

SUCH IS the legend of Daniel Webster and the great brook trout. Is there any truth to the story? In trying to answer that question, the place to begin is with the various accounts of the incident. For the most part, they are characterized by carelessness and slipshod scholarship. In *Bellport and Brookhaven,* Daniel Webster is identified as "a Senator from New York," which he never was.[2] The article in *Fly Fisherman* by James and Craig Wood relies on *Bellport and Brookhaven.*[3] Nicholas Karas claims that the record-breaking catch "was authenticated and witnessed" by many people, including Philip Hone, Parson King, and Martin Van Buren. Although Karas states that he used Hone's diary, he offers no citation to that document, or, for that matter, to anything else written by any of the alleged eyewitnesses to the dramatic event.[4] Like Karas, Ernest Schwiebert provides no citations to his many references. Schweibert, however, is somewhat more restrained than Karas. He calculates that reducing the size of the weathervane by a third would mean that the brook trout was approximately 25 inches in length and about 9 or 10 lbs. in weight, not 14½ lbs.[5] Charles

Eliot Goodspeed is the most scholarly of the authors, and the most cautious. He quotes an unidentified "prominent resident" of the town of South Haven as the source of the Webster trout story. Goodspeed goes on, however, to observe that two other early renditions of rumors about a big fish being taken in the Carmans River "make no mention of Webster's having caught the fish." Goodspeed even speculates that the trophy in question might have been a salmon, not a trout.[6]

The Webster trout story, in sum, is built on foundations of sand. Except for an oversized fish weathervane of uncertain origin, a Currier and Ives print showing a trout that hardly seems to have the girth required for a 14½ pounder,[7] and a name plate on a pew in Parson King's church bearing the inscription "The Suffolk Club," the evidence is thin. Even the name plate is not very helpful. According to the legend, Webster was a member of "The Suffolk Club."[8] The group, however, was not formed until 1858, and Webster left this world in 1852.

Being a Webster scholar, as well as a fly fisherman, I dearly hoped that the story was true. Accordingly, I made a search of the historical records, including the Papers of Daniel Webster at Dartmouth College. Drawn from many depositories, the Webster Papers at Dartmouth constitute the most complete compendium of Webster's correspondence, speeches, and writings in existence today.

The quest began on a promising note. Daniel Webster was in the right place at the right time. From about May 23 to June 6, 1827, he was in New York City. None of the letters he wrote during that time, however, contains a single word about angling. Rather, his correspondence from late May to early June 1827 is mainly concerned with law and politics. I also examined Webster's correspondence with those mentioned in the various accounts as having witnessed the taking of the great brook trout, regardless of chronology. No letters to or from Apaius

Enos, Reverend King, or Lige are contained in the Webster Papers. Webster did write one note to Philip Hone on April 30, 1831.[9] In this routine document, however, Webster merely informed Hone that he would not be in New York City long enough to attend a memorial dinner. In 1845, Webster sent two letters to Samuel Carman, but neither referred to the catching of an enormous trout.[10] On April 8, 1845, Webster told Carman that the weather was "so cold, I hardly know when I shall be your way," which indicates that he knew the tavern owner and considered making a trip to Fire Place. Nothing more, however, can be inferred from this interesting communication to Carman. Three Webster-Van Buren letters have been preserved, one undated and the others written in 1828 and 1836.[11] The undated document extended a dinner invitation to Webster, and the 1828 letter involved a legal case. The third letter, happily, did refer to a fish, but it was not a trout. On May 29, 1836, Webster invited Van Buren to a *"Salmon"* dinner. The fish, which Webster hoped had been "well preserved," had been given to him by a relative. None of the letters in the Webster Papers to or from the alleged eyewitnesses contained any reference to a large brook trout.

SINCE PHILIP HONE and Martin Van Buren play conspicuous roles in nearly all of the versions of the big fish story, their reminiscences also were scrutinized. None of the three published versions of Hone's famous diary, which he began in 1828, a year after the alleged occurrence, verifies the tale.[12] Indeed, one of Hone's diary entries seems to do the opposite. In April 1834, Hone observed that on a trip to the Carmans River he and his party "took some of the largest trout I ever saw," and the largest taken was 2 lbs. and 12 ounces—a long way from the assumed size of the great Webster trout.[13]

Since the manuscript of the Hone diary is more complete than the published versions and contains some items dating back to 1826, it also was examined. Hone did not actually begin to keep a systematic journal until 1828, and the documents prior to that time are mainly copies of speeches and lists of those invited to the dinner parties for which Philip Hone was justly famous. On May 31, 1827, about the time when the great brook trout was allegedly caught, Hone requested the presence of a number of eminent people. Daniel Webster was not among them. Webster's name first appeared as one of those invited for dinner on November 10, 1827. Whether he was actually a guest of Hone on the evening of November 10 is not known. More important, nothing whatsoever is mentioned in any of the 1827 documents about a massive brook trout that presumably was consumed at Delmonico's.[14] Hone, in fact, did not come into close contact with Daniel Webster until 1830, when he visited the Senator in Washington.[15] Thereafter, the two men developed a warm and lasting friendship, but this, of course, was years after the supposed incident on the Carmans River. The most colorful fishing excursion with Webster recorded in Hone's diary occurred in 1845, when Hone was a guest at Webster's estate in Marshfield. On July 9, the two men went fishing together aboard "the good sloop *Comet*" on Cape Cod Bay. The water was rough, and both Webster and Hone became seasick.[16]

In his autobiography, Martin Van Buren mentioned that he fished "in a pond a mile or two from my home," but he did not do so in the company of Daniel Webster.[17] It is, in fact, unlikely that Van Buren ever went fishing with Webster, for he did not like the statesman from Massachusetts. Webster, according to Van Buren, was a man of "ill will" toward Democrats.[18] Van Buren even bitterly characterized Webster as a person deficient "both in physical and moral courage."[19] Although they occasionally corresponded with one another and may have eaten a hopefully well-preserved salmon together, Martin Van Buren and Daniel Webster were political opponents who did not much care for one another.

So, where does that leave us? The story of Daniel Webster and the great brook trout seems to be apocryphal. Hoping to find historical evidence confirming what is an absolutely wonderful tale, I found none. Webster certainly was a fly fisherman, and a good one at that. For example, in June 1825 he took, by his own account, "26 trouts, all weighing 17 lb. 12 oz." (which meant that the trout averaged nearly 11 ounces each) from what he called "that chief of all brooks, Mashpee." He also had the familiar experience of losing the big one, which broke his line. Recalling that fine outing on the Mashpee, Webster stated that he had never "had so agreeable a days fishing," nor did he "ever expect such another."[20] Fortunately, he did have many other good days on the Mashpee and other trout streams, but there is no persuasive evidence that he ever landed a 14½ pounder on the Carmans River. Surely, he would have recorded such a gigantic catch for posterity in one of the hundreds of letters that he wrote after 1827, but, if he did, I have been unable to find it in the Webster Papers. I hope that a reader of *The American Fly Fisher* will prove me wrong by producing written historical evidence upholding the legend of Daniel Webster and the great brook trout, but I am afraid that the tale is what some people call a "fish story," which, I think, means a story too good to be true. §

---

[1] *The story of Daniel Webster and the great brook trout as recounted above is a composite drawn from the following sources: Stephanie S. Bigelow, compiler,* Bellport and Brookhaven: A Saga of the Sibling Hamlets at Old Purchase South *(New York, 1968), pp. 30-31, 46-47, 87; Charles Eliot Goodspeed,* Angling in America: Its Early History and Literature *(Boston, 1939), pp. 199-200; Nicholas Karas, "Daniel Webster Meets Another Kind of Devil,"* Rod & Gun *(Summer 1970); Ernest Schwiebert,* Trout *(2 vols.; New York, 1978), I, pp. 245-258; James and Craig Wood, "Long Island's Gift to American Trout Fishing: The Carmans River,"* Fly Fisherman, 7 *(Winter 1975), pp. 46-50.*
[2] Bellport and Brookhaven, *p. 31.*
[3] *See James and Craig Wood, "Long Island's Gift to American Trout Fishing," pp. 46-47.*
[4] *Karas, "Daniel Webster Meets Another Kind of Devil," p. 12.*

⁵ *Schwiebert,* Trout, *I, p. 248.*

⁶ *Goodspeed,* Angling in America, *pp. 199-200.*

⁷ *The Currier and Ives print, which was painted by Arthur Fitzwilliam Tait (1819-1905) in 1854, does not even mention Daniel Webster by name. It is entitled "Catching a Trout" and carries the caption "We Hab you Now, Sar." Although the angler playing the trout resembles Webster, I have found no evidence that Tait, one of America's greatest sporting artists, had the statesman from Massachusetts in mind. For information on the Currier and Ives print and Tait see Harry T. Peters,* Currier & Ives: Printmakers to the American People (*Garden City, New York, 1942*) *and E. Benezit,* Dictionnaire critique et documentaire des Peintres, Sculpteurs, Dessinateurs et Graveurs (*Paris, 1976*).

⁸ *See, for example, Schwiebert,* Trout, *I, p. 245.*

⁹ *Daniel Webster to Philip Hone, New York, April 30, 1831 (Dartmouth College-Webster Papers).*

¹⁰ *Webster to Samuel Carman, Boston, March 31, 1845; Webster to Carman, New York, April 8, 1845 (Suffolk County Historical Society, Riverhead, New York).*

¹¹ *Martin Van Buren to Webster, [n.p.], [n.d.] (Dartmouth College-Webster Papers); Webster to Van Buren, Boston, September 27, 1828 (Massachusetts Historical Society-Van Buren Papers); Webster to Van Buren [n.p.], May 29, 1836 (Phillips Exeter Academy).*

¹² *Allan Nevins, ed.,* The Diary of Philip Hone, 1828-1851 (*2 vols.; New York, 1927); Nevins, ed.,* The Diary of Philip Hone, 1828-1851 (*rev. and enlarged ed.; New York, 1936); Bayard Tuckerman, ed.,* The Diary of Philip Hone, 1828-1851 (*2 vols.; New York, 1889*).

¹³ *Tuckerman, ed.,* The Diary of Philip Hone, *I, p. 102.*

¹⁴ *Philip Hone Diary. Volume I: January 17, 1826-April 4, 1829. New York Historical Society.*

¹⁵ *See Nevins, ed.,* The Diary of Philip Hone (*rev. and enlarged ed.*), *p. 23.*

¹⁶ Ibid., *pp. 736-738.*

¹⁷ *John C. Fitzpatrick, ed.,* The Autobiography of Martin Van Buren (*Washington, 1920*), *p. 536.*

¹⁸ Ibid., *p. 561.*

¹⁹ Ibid., *p. 662.*

²⁰ *Webster to Henry Cabot, June 4, [1825] as printed in Charles M. Wiltse and Harold D. Moser, eds.,* The Papers of Daniel Webster, Correspondence, Volume 2, 1825-1829 (*Hanover, New Hampshire, 1976*), *pp. 51-52.*

# First You Get a Fly Rod

*Geoffrey Norman*

T HE ROD, like everything else packed in the back of my car, was brand new. I had taken it out of the aluminum carrying tube perhaps a dozen times, first to admire it and then to take it down to the park where a friendly young man who belonged to one of the city's casting clubs showed me how to use it properly. But that had been casting to plastic rings anchored in a shallow, lifeless pond where a man on some kind of desperate night errand had been recently murdered. Now, after owning the rod for almost six months, I was going to use it where it was built to be used—on a trout stream.

Now, I was no kid. I was in my late twenties, a veteran, and a rising young magazine editor. I owned my automobile outright, and I played the stock market and bet the NFL football games. Nor was I an absolute novice as an angler, since I had caught fish as exotic as wahoo and northern pike. I was not even an absolute newcomer to fly-fishing. I had caught largemouth bass as large as seven pounds on an old fiberglass rod that disappeared after I went into the service. And a few months earlier I had caught a five-pound smallmouth one memorable morning on a borrowed fly rod up in Canada. A few minutes before I caught the fish, I saw a bald eagle, the first that I had seen wild in twenty years. It was one of those interludes that come to you in fishing and are with you the rest of your life.

But I had never used a fly rod on a trout stream. There were good reasons for this; some obvious and sound, others not so obvious but, I think, just as sound. Maybe even more so. I had done most of my growing up in the South, the greatest part of it on the Gulf Coast where there were simply no trout to be caught. So I learned to fish for bass. And when I thought I was good enough, I moved up from bait-casting to fly-casting. I got to be pretty good with a frog-patterned popping bug around a lily pad. It was one of the joys of my young life.

In those days, kids read about their enthusiasms. If they were big sports fans, there were magazines full of articles about their favorite athletes, along with full-page color pictures that you could tear out of the magazine and hang on your wall. If you were hot on cars, there were magazines that carried all the latest information on the new models and advertisements for tools and kits to help you rebuild the old ones. And if you cared about hunting and fishing, there were some fine publications full of stories and tips, advertisements to drool over, and even an occasional brush with literature. These days, when specialization is the word, it is hard to remember that *Field & Stream* published *The Old Man and the Boy* by Robert Ruark as a serial. My father and I would try to beat each other to the mailbox to get at the next installment. Writers as fine as Vance Bourjaily and Phillip Wylie used to appear regularly in the outdoor magazines.

And I read them avidly, like so many young boys of my generation. After a while I did not pay that much attention to the articles about bass fishing. I was getting to that point where I had heard most of it—and even to the point where I thought I knew more than some of the writers. But I read about trout and salmon eagerly, and I began to think of that as "real fishing." For one thing, the tackle was so fine. Split-cane rods instead of the tough old fiberglass tool that I had picked up for less than twenty dollars. Trout fishermen still wrote about silk lines and gut leaders. They had formulas for leader tapers— some of their leaders ran fifteen feet—and they carried these lovely willow creels. Bass fishermen used five or six feet of available monofilament line for a leader and put the fish they caught on a metal stringer. They could have been catfish.

Then there were the flies. Wets and drys in all sorts of patterns and sizes. A good trout-fishing writer could give you five different flies in the course of his opening paragraph. By the time you finished the article, you would be exposed to a dozen or more. And the confidence with which he selected his flies; changing whenever he got a refusal. It was too much for a boy who owned perhaps ten cork popping bugs that he divided into two categories—big ones and small ones.

Furthermore, trout fishermen went to the best places. Cold northern streams where there were no other fishermen, not to mention the water skiers, duck hunters, and alligator poachers that bass fishermen often had to put up with. The trout men did some of their fishing in places where English was not spoken. And on this continent, their rivers had names like the Snake and the Rogue.

In ten years of reading those magazines I developed a healthy inferiority complex. I would, I decided, never be a trout fisherman. The game was too refined for the likes of me, who sometimes—the shame of it—would put on a *very* small bug and spend an hour or two catching a stringer of bluegills. I would never understand opera, either, or read Homer in the original Greek; some things were just not in the cards. I sup-

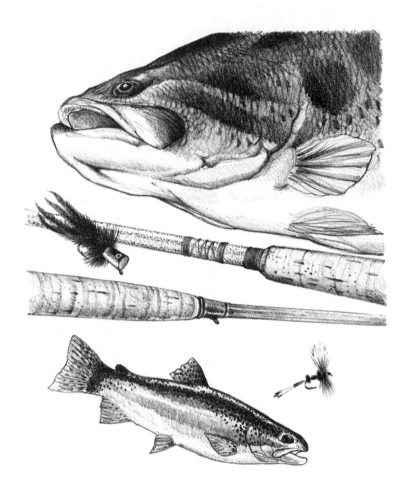

posed I resigned myself to all of this at some time or another. The worst part of it was knowing that I would never feel first-hand what was described in some of my favorite writing. Not to be able to live what Nick Adams lived in "Big Two Hearted River" seemed a real loss.

And probably I never would have fished for trout if it had not been for the rod that lay in the back of the car, now, with all the other brand-new gear, some of it still smelling like the fishing department of Abercrombie's where it all came from, including the rod.

I had bought all of that gear—except the rod. It had been given to me by a man who will always be a friend and who taught me an awful lot when I still had so much to learn that I thought I knew it all. He was my boss as well as my friend, and he handled both roles superbly. He was a city boy; Jewish and raised in the Bronx. He had a quick mind and was sincerely curious about those things he had not seen up close. So he asked me about the South, and I tried to tell him about it, just as he tried to tell me about the city. Then he traveled to Alabama with me on two or three occasions, and I spent some time with him in New York. It was an odd friendship, but solid and genuine. We liked each other.

We also did favors for each other, and one day he decided that something I had done for him called for some sort of special thanks. It wasn't really that much of a favor, but he had a sense of honor fierce as any Southerner's, and he felt obliged to do more than say "thanks." Since I had just come back from a trip to Canada and some fine smallmouth fishing and had talked about it until all my friends were bored with it, he decided to get me a fly rod.

So he went to Abercrombie's on his lunch hour one day and asked the clerk for the best fly rod they carried. Something fine. Being from the Bronx and having never been fishing in his entire life, he wasn't able to answer the clerk's questions. He simply said he wanted the best. Fishing poles were fishing poles. What's to select?

He came into my office after lunch and handed me one of the last Orvis rods built by Wes Jordan, the master builder. It was their basic trout rod, eight feet long, about four ounces, made of split bamboo with the deep finish that is characteristic of Orvis rods. I slipped the rod out of the aluminum tube and then the cloth bag and joined it at the ferrule, which locked up snugger than my old fiberglass stick ever had. I gave it a little action with my wrist, and the rod felt strong and responsive. I knew that I had something special in my hand.

So I thanked my friend, and he smiled with the satisfaction that comes from giving a gift that hits home. I put the rod up in the corner of my office and looked at it for the rest of the day. That night I took it home to my apartment. And I decided that I would have to learn how to become a trout fisherman even if I was old and unworthy and had been weaned on bass and bluegills. I could not own a rod that fine and not use it . . . and use it well. The physical gift and the human impulse behind the giving of it both demanded nothing less.

It was November, so I had a few months to learn about trout fishing before I could actually go out and do it. Eager as I was to use the rod, I looked on the next few months as something of a grace period, and I started in on my homework.

I started buying books and reading them at night trying to learn the actual meaning of terms that had always been obscure. Just what in the hell was a 6X tippet? A roll cast? A drag-free float? And so on and so forth. I studied and I learned and I wondered if I could ever put all of it together. I decided to save the entire business of flies for last. I'd never be able to learn all those patterns from books. When the time came, I would buy some flies and learn them as I fished with them.

Now, there are a lot of books published about fly-fishing and a lot of them are very smug, erudite, and daunting to the man who sits in his city apartment reading them and trying to learn the fundamentals. A few of the books I picked up were absolutely infuriating, written by men who seemed more interested in protecting the mysteries than in unraveling them. Their prose was prolix, and their tone was condescending, and I finally said to hell with them.

86

I settled on a few congenial souls who seemed to think that fishing was something that one first does for pleasure and never for status. The books of A. J. McClane, Ray Bergman, and Peter Barrett were very helpful. Charles Waterman's *Modern Fresh and Salt Water Fly Fishing* was the closest thing I had that winter to a companion. Chatty, wise, and reassuring. And, praise the Lord, a book that gave bass fishing with the fly rod a place right up there on the front of the bus. After I'd read Waterman's book two or three times I began to feel like I might be able to do right by my new rod after all.

Spring was getting close when I discovered the casting club and the helpful young man who showed me how to smooth out a very rough stroke and make my brand new, peach-colored fly line turn over like it was blown by a soft wind instead of shot from a gun. I began to go to the park with my rod at dawn, before there was any traffic or any hecklers, and I would cast for an hour, trying to imagine how it would be on moving water. After I lost my concentration and got lazy, I would break the rod down and put it back in its case, go home to the apartment and change for work. Every day, I was thinking more and more about Opening Day. Up in Michigan.

I did not know where to go. Just for fun one day I studied a map of Michigan until I found the Two Hearted River. It looked to be seven or eight hundred miles from Chicago and so far north that it might still be covered with ice on Opening Day. I needed something a little closer to home. So I called a poet I knew who lived in Michigan and loved to fish and asked him where I should go. "Baldwin," he said. "The Pere Marquette River." I went back to the map, found it, and planned my route. This was probably a month before Opening Day.

The next week I went to the catalogs and back to Abercrombie's and bought waders and a vest and a leader wallet and all kinds of fly boxes . . . things that I used once or twice and that have followed me through three moves and have never been used again and never will be. I don't need a leader wallet any more or a device to help me knot my fly on. But this was going to be my first season, with my new rod, and I wanted to be ready.

THE SEASON OPENED on a Saturday in early May. On Friday I left work early, and with my car full of new gear, drove to Baldwin, some two hundred twenty miles away. It was before the fifty-five speed limit, and I made it in less than four hours. There was still a little light when I got to town. I studied the river from the bridge. It looked high and dark, not at all like the trout streams of my reading or my imagination. It didn't even look safe to wade.

I got a cabin on the banks of the river, and that night I went through all of my tackle. I sorted a few flies that I had bought from Orvis in one of those basic selections. I studied each fly and tried to learn how to recognize it. I tied up some extra leaders, which more than filled my leader wallet. I must have had thirty leaders. I greased my fly line even though it had not spent a total of five hours on water. I tried to sleep, but did not. Instead, I listened to the river and tried to imagine that I could hear the water level falling.

In the morning I bought a license and some flies. The man who sold me the flies had been fishing the river for more than twenty years. He had moved up from Detroit, and he ran a little shop. When I told him how raw I was, he helped me and sold me some flies that he said would work if there were any hatches, which he doubted since the river was so high. I thanked him and said I would be back. I was . . . to the tune of several hundred dollars over the next five years.

I don't have to tell anyone who has ever fly-fished anything more about my day. It was awful. I fell in the river before I'd made twenty casts. I spent hours freeing my fly from the alders that grew along the banks of the river and that I'd never had to take into consideration when I was casting from a platform in a city park. I could not master moving water, locate fish, identify insects, or get warm. When I got back to my little cabin at dark, thinking only of a hot shower and a glass of dark whiskey, I felt like I had let my rod down.

The next day was more of the same, less the dunking. I considered it some sort of victory that I had learned to walk. One of these days perhaps I would learn to run. Now, if I could just keep the fly out of the tag alders and get a nice drag-free drift from time to time, maybe I could actually catch a fish, though I had not seen the first rise or, for that matter, the first hatching mayfly. My spirits were as low as the sullen sky that stretched west and north across all the vastness of Lake Michigan.

Then, an hour before I had to leave the water and Baldwin and head back to the city, I caught a fish. I was casting a little Royal Coachman that had gotten soaked and I hadn't bothered to dry and refloat. It did not seem worth the trouble. I was flicking the little fly out ahead of me, downstream, as I made my way back to the car. It had been a sorry baptism for my new rod.

I almost missed the strike. In fact, I would have if I had not been fishing downstream and the line had not been pulled tight. My presentation, such as it was, could not have been further from a drag-free drift. The strike of the fish set the hook, and when I realized what had happened, I played my catch with all the care I could manage. I didn't want to lose this fish, no matter how artlessly he had been hooked.

It was a rainbow, all six inches of him. One thing I had learned studying those books was how to identify the various trout, and this was a rainbow. I admired him long as I dared then popped the hook loose with my brand-new forceps and let him swim away. I felt much better. In fact, I felt the most

comforting of all the emotions—hope. We had to start somewhere, my rod and I, and this was it. With a miserable weekend and one tiny trout, hooked by accident.

I went back to Baldwin almost every weekend of that trout
season, and I got an education. Within a couple of months, I
was catching small fish fairly regularly. And I was losing fewer
than six flies a day in the tag alders, and I never fell down anymore. I could keep forty feet of line out, and I could actually
make a kind of amateur's curve cast to achieve the fabled drag-
free drift. I was beginning to feel worthy of the rod. Maybe I
would rise above my poor origins.

Sometime in the middle of the summer I was persuaded to
go out at night, which was, they said, the only time to catch
big trout on the Pere Marquette. My friend who had come up
from Detroit to open the little shop obligingly sold me a dozen
flies for night fishing. Any one of them would cover the palm
of your hand, and the hooks were so big they looked danger-
ous. I still hit myself in the head with my fly once or twice a
day and I knew that if it happened with one of these beauties I
would need to make a trip to the emergency room. But I was
game.

And behold, I actually caught a fish that could be called
"big" by the relaxed standards of the Pere Marquette. It would
have been merely a "nice fish" west of the Mississippi, but here
it was a little better than that. The fish ran off line and worked
all over the pool I was fishing. He felt very strong in the darkness and he looked bigger than he was when I finally got him in
the beam of my light. I felt like I had arrived.

So I took a trip north to visit the Two Hearted. Actually,
if you want to fish the river that Nick Adams fished in the famous story, then you go to the Fox; Hemingway used the name
of the other river for reasons that are obvious. But it was a sort
of pilgrimage, this trip, and by the end of the summer, I felt I
had earned it.

The fishing was slow, but I didn't really care. The countryside was magnificent, full of meaning beyond its undeniable beauty. I had a memorable three or four days, and thought once or twice about what a splendid gift the rod had been.

I had learned an awful lot in less than a year. Enough to make me a trout fisherman and give me a pastime that will last me, I trust, as long as I live. I would never say that I learned the best way. In fact, I would listen respectfully to anyone who wanted to say that I learned in the worst way. Books by themselves are not good teachers. And trial and error is a sure way to learn bad habits, which I did and am still having trouble with. But I was never going to learn unless I learned that way. And I still remember that summer when I would drive to the Pere Marquette on Fridays and take a little cabin by the river and fall asleep thinking of the next day's fishing. I learned more and caught less than I have most summers since then. There were times that still live vividly in my memory. The time I worked a rising fish through five fly changes before I got him to take. Another time when I stumbled on a great hatch of some kind of dark late-season mayfly, tied on an Adams, and took my limit for the first time ever. My first look at a really big fish, a steelhead, late that fall, when the leaves had changed color and you could hear the occasional blast of a grouse hunter's shotgun off in the distance. I wouldn't have had any of that if it had not been for the rod, which is still my favorite among an accumulation of speedier cane models, graphites, and even boron/graphites. The rod is one of the few things I own that I am genuinely sentimental about, and I wouldn't take anything for it. It was my teacher. §

# Burt's Gun

*William G. Tapply*

RICK SNAPPED the little shotgun to his shoulder and led an imaginary woodcock across my living-room wall. "Comes up nice," he said. He rubbed his thumb along the side of the safety, where the bluing has worn shiny. "Not exactly mint."

"No," I said. "She's traveled many miles."

"Still . . . a Parker double. Twenty-gauge. What's her grade?"

"VH."

Rick nodded and cocked an eye at me. "For sale?"

I laughed. "Hardly. It's an heirloom."

"But I thought . . ."

"Oh, Dad's still very much alive. It wasn't his. Belonged to an old guy I used to hunt with. Name of Burt Spiller."

"Not *the* Burt Spiller?"

"Himself," I said.

"The 'Poet Laureate' of the ruffed grouse," mused Rick. "All those great stories. You knew Burt Spiller?"

"Like I said. I hunted with him."

BURTON L. SPILLER WAS BORN in 1886 in the tiny seacoast town of Wells, Maine. Seven years later he blasted a grouse from the lower branches of an oak tree with his father's hammer-action 10-gauge double. The bruised shoulder and nosebleed he suffered from the recoil failed to discourage him, and he tromped the New England meadows and woodlands for more than seven decades before he took off his hunting boots for the last time at the end of the 1964 season.

Burt Spiller may well have invested more hours—and surely more seasons—in grouse hunting than any man in history. When he was a teenager Burt accepted the invitation to join up with two local market hunters. Grouse were abundant in southern Maine in those days. The three skilled and dedicated gunners moved fifty or more grouse on a typical day's hunt. But if Burt discovered the tricks by which men can outwit grouse, his two years as a commercial grouse hunter also taught him "the difference between a sportsman and that reprehensible thing I was fast becoming," as he said in his first published story, "His Majesty, the Grouse," which appeared in *Field & Stream* half a century ago. So he "bought a registered bird dog and became a sportsman."

My first ten years of grouse hunting were Burt's last ten, and we shared them. Every October and November Saturday morning for the decade between 1954 and 1964, Dad and I pulled up in front of Burt's house in East Rochester, New Hampshire. His gun and shooting vest waited for us on his front porch. Burt always had his boots laced. "I'm ready," he'd grin.

I was fourteen and he was nearly seventy when I began hunting with him. His only concession to age was the hearing aid he wore, one of the old-fashioned kind with a little button in one ear and wires running to a battery pack in his shirt pocket. It must have been a terrible handicap for a partridge hunter. "I can hear the birds flush," he explained, "and I can hear you when you yell 'Mark!' But I don't know where to look."

So Burt didn't shoot very often. He didn't seem to mind. Even on the good days, when the woodcock flights were in the Bullring and Mankiller covers, and when the Henhouse and Long Walk In covers each held a brood of grouse, and when Dad and I might go through a box of shells each, Burt's gunbarrels often remained clean. Yet when we dropped him off at his house at the end of the day he'd always say, "A wonderful hunt. See you next Saturday."

When he could see a flying partridge, though, Burt Spiller was a master wing-shot. Once during the first season I hunted with him, he and I were strolling down an old logging road together on the way out of our Orchard Hillside cover. The tall beeches along either side of the road still held their leaves, and evergreens hugged close to the ruts we were following, so that it seemed as if we were walking through a green-and-gold tun-

nel. The hunt had ended, and our guns hung at our sides. Somewhere off to our left Dad and our hell-for-leather setter, Duke, were taking their own route. We could hear the dog's bell and Dad's occasional shouts to him.

Then he yelled, "Mark! Your way!"

I was standing slightly behind Burt, so I could see his gun come up as the grouse darted across the 10-foot opening of the roadway 30 yards in front of us. When Burt shot, the bird crumpled, its momentum tumbling it into the hemlocks. We found it stone dead. Burt picked it up and stroked its breast feathers and fanned its tail.

"I'm sorry," he said to me. "I should have let you take him."

I couldn't have made that shot once in a hundred chances. Burt knew that, I'm sure.

He had hands like a blacksmith's—which he once had been—cracked and hardened from digging and sorting the gladiolus bulbs that he raised commercially, so his skin looked like the bark of a lightning-struck apple tree. But when he rubbed his finger alongside the trigger guard of his beautiful Parker, or stroked the ruff of a warm grouse, one could imagine him fashioning sweet-singing violins—which was something else he did.

He's best remembered, of course, for the stories he crafted. Their themes were all similar: the hero was usually "Thunder King," the grouse, often the dog, and only rarely the man. Before I ever hunted with him I had read all of Burt's tales I could lay my hands on, so I knew him even before I met him. And I felt he knew me, too. "Other boys of my acquaintance," he wrote in "His Majesty, the Grouse," "might content themselves with slaying elephants and lions and other inconsequential members of the animal kingdom, but I wanted none of that in mine. Nothing but the lordly pa'tridge would satisfy me."

Or me.

Burt was an old-fashioned man. He refused to profane the Sabbath by hunting, even though New Hampshire law allowed it. Neither Dad nor I ever heard him utter even the mildest curse, or speak critically of another, or express anger. He was a teetotaler and a devoted family man. But he had a wry Yankee sense of humor. He enjoyed a joke, especially if it was on him.

From the top of the hill along the road between the School-house and Tripwire covers near the little township of Gilmanton Iron Works stretches a magnificent vista of the southern New Hampshire countryside. In the fall it's washed with crimson and gold. Sparkling lakes and ponds nestle among the foothills of the White Mountains. Dad always pulled over to the side there and nudged Burt, who'd grin in anticipation of their joke.

"That's where we'll build our cabin when we get old," Dad would say, pointing to a spot under an ancient sugar maple. "We'll watch the seasons go by, gamble a lot, and have all the wild wimmin and rye whiskey we want."

"Especially the whiskey," Burt would always say.

When I first began to hunt grouse and woodcock, it was a deadly serious business of finding and flushing and shooting. I measured the success of the hunt by the numbers. I was a teenager, and I didn't know any better. It took several seasons of hunting with Burt Spiller and Dad, and the rereading of Burt's stories, before it came into perspective for me, so that I could say at the end of every day, "A wonderful hunt." And mean it.

ON THE FIRST SATURDAY of October 1964, Burt and Dad and I stepped from the car at our First Chance cover. First Chance was a short hunt. "Just right for getting out the kinks," Burt always said. A grouse lived there, and a few native woodcock usually twittered away before we were done.

We slid our shotguns from their cases and crammed our vest pockets with shells while Duke whined and strained at the end of his check cord.

"Let me heft your gun, Bill," said Burt.

I handed him the Savage single-shot 20-gauge that had cost me more hours of lawn mowing and weed pulling than I care to remember. Burt lifted it to his shoulder and swung it against the sky.

"Feels good," he said. "Mind if I try it?"

I shrugged. "Sure. Go ahead."

"Here," he said. "You carry mine. If you don't mind."

He placed his Parker in both of my hands. "I don't mind," I said. I didn't understand why he'd want to try my Savage. It wasn't much of a gun. But I couldn't turn down the opportunity to carry that beautiful Parker just once.

We climbed a stone wall and crossed a frosted meadow until we came to an alder run. A stream trickled through it. Beyond rose a hillside overgrown with apples and briers. Burt followed the field edge, Dad slogged the mucky alder bottom, and I kept pace on the hillside, praying for a chance to try Burt's gun.

We found the grouse at home in First Chance that day. He scuttled ahead of the dog until he was pinned at the edge of an opening ahead of me. I came up quickly behind Duke's point. The Parker felt light in my hands. The bird exploded from under a clump of juniper, angled up to the tops of the alders, then slid swiftly back toward the old orchard. The Parker, I discovered that morning, shot exactly where I aimed it—in that case, several feet behind the fleeing partridge.

When we got out of the car at the next cover, Burt picked up my Savage. "I didn't get to shoot it back there," he said. "Mind if I try it again?"

I hesitated, then took his Parker, "Okay." I said.

We carried each other's gun for the rest of that Saturday. And when we dropped Burt off that afternoon, he left the Parker in the car and took the Savage with him. "You use it," he said. "I won't be hunting tomorrow."

Thus did Burt Spiller's gun pass into my hands—in Burt's

way, without ceremony, without giving me the chance to say "thank you," and therefore without his needing to acknowledge that he had indeed bestowed upon me a priceless gift.

Later that season—Burt's last in the woods, as he may have suspected—we were hunting Tripwire, a hellish hillside of bramble and blowdown. The woodcock, by then, had moved south. Grouse were scarce. Dad and I plowed through the thick of it, while Burt took the only route his seventy-eight-year-old legs permitted, the old roadway several hundred yards off to our right. Duke roamed somewhere ahead of us. Then we heard the rumble of a flushing grouse.

"Damn that dog!" muttered Dad. Then he yelled, "Burt! Mark!"

Many seconds seemed to elapse before we heard Burt's shot. "He got him!" said Dad.

"Aw, come on. How can you tell?"

"You can tell by the sound of the shot," Dad replied, smiling. "You wait."

We cut back toward the roadway and came to it behind Burt. He was trudging ahead of us, his old legs slowly taking him up the incline of the road. My Savage hung at his side from his right hand. A ruffed grouse dangled by its legs from his left.

Burt quit hunting at the end of that season. He lived for nine more years, raising gladioli and carving violins and writing more tales of the outdoors. I like to think that he savored a special memory of his last grouse, which he shot with my gun.

And when he died in 1973, that old single-shot Savage came back to me with Burt's instructions: "For Bill's son."

"So ACTUALLY," I told Rick, "I own two of Burt Spiller's shotguns."

"Not for sale, eh?" nodded Rick.

"No way," I said. "But if you take special care of it I'll let you borrow this book."

From my bookcase I slid my copy of *Grouse Feathers*, by Burton L. Spiller, Crown's facsimile reproduction of the Derrydale original.

Rick opened the book and peered at the inscription. "I can't read it," he said.

"Burt was eighty-six when he wrote it," I said. "His hand was pretty shaky. It took me a while to decipher. Here's what it says."

And I read Burt Spiller's words to my friend:

*To Bill—*
*While listening in on grouse conversations*
*This is, I find, their chief complaint:*
*Not only do you always bust 'em,*
*But often bust 'em where they ain't.*
*From Burt.*

"Did you?" asked Rick.

"Did I what?"

"Bust 'em where they weren't?"

"Couldn't then, can't now," I said. "I'm a lousy wingshot, even with Burt's gun. Actually, that inscription is one of the last—and most far-fetched—pieces of grouse-shooting fiction Burt Spiller ever wrote." §

# Aldo Leopold:
# A Durable Scale of Values

*Boyd Gibbons*

ALDO LEOPOLD has been referred to as a naturalist. He was an extraordinary one. But that's like describing Lincoln as a politician. You have only part of the man. Leopold was also a remarkable craftsman, a professional forester who saw more than the forest, one of the first professors of wildlife management, and an uncommon conservationist. These too are but arcs of his circumference.

Go to his essays and journals: *A Sand County Almanac* and *Round River*. There is the center of the man. Aldo Leopold elevated ecology to philosophy and literature. Were that his sole achievement, it would be enough. If the passenger pigeon had to pass into oblivion, God knows it went out on a dazzling requiem:

*Men still live who, in their youth, remember pigeons. Trees still live who, in their youth, were shaken by a living wind. But a decade hence only the oldest oaks will remember, and at long last only the hills will know. . . . The pigeon was a biological storm. . . . he lived by the intensity of his desire for clustered grape and bursting beechnut, and by his contempt of miles and seasons.*

His former students at the University of Wisconsin still remember Leopold as "the professor," but he was ever the inquiring student, burrowing into histories of the West, and accounts of exploration—the narrative of the expedition of Coronado, the diaries of Lewis and Clark. He underlined facts—where the grizzly had been—filling his various journals that over the years included gleanings from Cicero—"It is doubted whether a man ever brings his faculties to bear with their full force on a subject until he writes upon it"—Thoreau, Lincoln, Edwin Arlington Robinson, Milton, Keats, Shakespeare, Epicurus, Xenophon, Tacitus, Plutarch, Isaiah. His tools, always sharp, were extensions of his mind: eye, pencil, ax, shovel, his dogs (well, not always his dogs—Gus once pointed "pheasants" and retrieved a piglet).

Leopold drew his strength from marsh, farm, prairie, rimrock, wilderness, his biases evident: "a completely industrialized United States is of no consequence to me." He helped found the Wilderness Society. He defined wilderness, gave it meaning long before Congress gave it protection.

Leopold was a man of the camp fragrant with blue smoke of mesquite. He hunted, he fished, drawing from a farmer, from the scratchings of grouse, what was not found in books. One of his journals contains this note about quail: "One cock flew into elm and defecated on my face; could identify blackberry skins in dropping." Leopold spent a lifetime reading animal sign, reading the landscape, reading civilization—a lifetime, his son Luna would observe, developing perception. A perception that heard music from the wild goose, then supplied the lyrics:

*In dire necessity somebody might write another Iliad, or paint an 'Angelus,' but fashion a goose? . . . If, then, we can* live without goose music, we may as well do away with stars, or sunsets, or Iliads. *But the point is that we would be fools to do away with any of them.*

Of what economic value are geese or grizzlies? Next to nothing, said Leopold, so let us not "invent subterfuges to give [them] economic importance." Their continued existence must rest on other reasons. He did not disdain laws or other political means to achieve conservation, but he did have the sense to see their limitations, that if "there is as yet no social stigma in the possession of a gullied farm, a wrecked forest," all our controls and subsidies are but futile attempts at repairing damage—bad economics and bad land use.

Aldo Leopold tied the future of the natural world—what he called land, what we now call environment—to man's conscience. From someone with a less rigorous intellect, Leopold's "land ethic" might have fluttered into preciousness or preaching. But he was neither precious nor a preacher. His message—the keel of his thinking—was not a call to worship, but rather a gentle plea for self-inquiry:

*There is as yet no ethic dealing with man's relation to land and to the animals and plants which grow upon it. . . . The land-relation is still strictly economic, entailing privileges but not obligations. . . . Obligations have no meaning without conscience, and the problem we face is the extension of the social conscience from people to land.*

*No important change in ethics was ever accomplished without an internal change in our intellectual emphasis, loyalties, affections, and convictions. The proof that conservation has not yet touched these foundations of conduct lies in the fact that philosophy and religion have not yet heard of it. In our attempt to make conservation easy, we have made it trivial.*

Times and environmental attitudes, we might say, have changed. Do we not now have environmental-impact statements to guide decisions? We do indeed—by the ton—but they seem to guide mostly the fortunes of the consultants who prepare them.

Look to the land. The wheat fields of the Palouse in Washington still erode as in Leopold's time. We have more places labeled wilderness (and more people to label them), but fewer that are wild. How falls the rain? By the pH.

There are disciples who deify Leopold, who refuse to see that he was mortal—of modest height, blue eyes, a balding brow, a prominent nose, full lips, and a flat stomach—that he went to bed early, leaving visitors to chat with his wife, and that before he learned to respect the role of predators he often shot hawks on sight. At a recent Sierra Club conference, after a former student of his had related Leopold's shift in attitude toward predators, a man took the stage and shouted, "You are sullying the name of a great man!" Leopold dipped into the Bible, but he kept his distance from churches. He would have withdrawn from attempts to enshrine him.

Leopold died of a heart attack in 1948 at 61, while helping a neighbor fight a grass fire near his weekend shack in Wisconsin. *It is warm behind the driftwood now, for the wind has gone with the geese. So would I—if I were the wind.*

To FIND THE MAN, start with the boy. He was born Rand Aldo Leopold in Burlington, Iowa, January 11, 1887. His grandfather, Charles Starker, a German architect from Stuttgart, owned the local bank, a company that made handsome hardwood desks, and an impressive home high on a bluff overlooking the Mississippi River—for young Aldo a satisfying aristocratic milieu.

"Aldo was the apple of his mother's eye," his brother Frederic told me. "We didn't hold it against him, but her preference for him embarrassed Father a bit, and sometimes even embarrassed Aldo."

Every Saturday the cook baked two cakes, but before they

could be served, Aldo would help himself. His mother padlocked the cake boxes. Aldo filed off the locks.

"Mother never even considered chastising him," said his sister Marie, who still lives in the old house on the lip of the bluff, Frederic next door. "As a boy, Aldo didn't talk a lot, but he was a smart student. He liked a dance if pretty girls were there, but if he didn't want to go to a party, he would just say, 'No, I've got something else to do.' We all played golf, but Aldo wouldn't. He considered it foolishness. He would go for a walk."

With his mother's opera glasses and canister for collecting plants, Aldo would ride the streetcar to the end of the line and disappear into the woods. Often as not he carried his shotgun and a notebook, the beginnings of his prolific and literate journals.

"Aldo read a great deal as a boy," said Frederic, "his preference being books on wood lore. Even then he was becoming skillful at reading sign, knowing what the animals were eating, what had been chasing them, who was eating whom. He seemed to have gotten this love of the outdoors from Dad."

On dark fall mornings young Aldo and his father pulled on hip boots by gaslight, then clumped down the hill to the railway station for a breakfast of pork and beans and a baked apple. The train took them across the Mississippi to a marsh where, crouched on a muskrat house, they awaited the whiffling of ducks. In the off-season they would explore the marsh, find a mink den, see what the mink had been eating.

Long before federal law prohibited hunting during the nesting season, Aldo's father concluded that it was wrong to do so and ended his shooting in winter, a lesson in sportsmanship not lost on his son.

"Aldo was tremendously sensitive," said Frederic, "and very anxious to be ethical—that was extremely important to him. He had no patience with bad intentions or bad ethics. He was a perfectionist."

In 1903, before Leopold arrived, the headmaster of the Lawrenceville School in New Jersey received this communication from the Burlington High School principal: "He is as earnest a boy as we have in school. . . . painstaking in his work. . . . Moral character above reproach."

At Lawrenceville, Aldo got the reputation of being bright and talented—a "shark." He was also something of a dude. Much to his father's distress, Aldo acquired a taste for Brooks Brothers suits, expensive shoes, and hand-tailored shirts, a taste that would accompany him to Yale's Sheffield Scientific School, and, with variations, well beyond.

In early July 1909 with a Master of Forestry degree in his portmanteau, Aldo Leopold stepped off the train at Albuquerque. The United States Forest Service had recently been established, and to it came an elite cadre of foresters from Yale. The Forest Service promptly sent Leopold into the Blue Range of the Arizona Territory. His facility for cruising timber was quickly eclipsed by his awe for cowboys, their ability to travel light and cook well. He imagined bowlegs and sought something to put them around: "Bought—grey horse from F. E. Irwin . . . $70 down . . . $65 from bank." He soon reached the end of his salary. He picked up his pen: "My dear Papa. . . ." Father resisted, remembering the Brooks raids into his capital. Mother prevailed. Aldo bought a rope, a .30-30 carbine, a revolver, boots, batwing chaps, and a hat that practically shaded his horse. Off he rode.

Leopold's trail eventually intersected the vast sheep lands of the Lunas, Spanish aristocrats of the New Mexico Territory. His eyes alighted on Estella Bergere (her mother was a Luna), whose dark eyes and traditional values lifted him out of the saddle and into marriage. Appointed to supervise the Carson

National Forest in northern New Mexico, he reviewed his rangers' diaries, entering "Bully!" in the margins when talent struck his eye. At Tres Piedras, Aldo built a frame house, and he and Estella settled in.

But a storm caught Leopold in the back-country, and acute nephritis—after a cold night in a wet bedroll—ended his days as a back-country forester, and almost ended him. Sick for more than a year, he recuperated at home in Burlington.

Aldo Leopold returned to Albuquerque and the Forest Service a more reflective man. Gone was the cowboy bravado, the chinking of spurs. He administered grazing permits and was soon absorbed in his elemental affection: wildlife ("Arrested Arno Blueher for killing kingbird . . . fined $50 and costs"). He stumped the region to form associations for the protection of game. On weekends, his shotgun and son Starker strapped behind, he bicycled down to the cottonwoods to hunt quail and dove, or try for ducks on the Rio Grande.

He showed Starker how cattle were destroying quail cover; they put up small fences to detour cows. Aldo saw a hawk pin a quail in an *Atriplex* bush. Shot the hawk. Saw a roadrunner with a quail chick in its beak. Shot the roadrunner. Predators kill our game, he told Starker. Wolves, too—they eat our deer. Eradicate them. Leopold wounded a wolf in a boggy meadow, and when she charged, he had to jam the gunstock in her mouth to evade the teeth.

Years later, in his essay "Thinking Like a Mountain," Leopold admitted his error about predators.

*We reached the old wolf in time to watch a fierce green fire dying in her eyes. I realized then, and have known ever since, that there was something new to me in those eyes—something known only to her and to the mountain. I was young then, and full of trigger itch; I thought that because fewer wolves meant more deer, that no wolves would mean hunters' para-*

*dise. But after seeing the green fire die, I sensed that neither the wolf nor the mountain agreed with such a view.*

For some time he had been urging the Forest Service to set aside roadless areas as wilderness, particularly the Gila in New Mexico. In 1924, as Leopold was leaving the Southwest for Madison, Wisconsin, the Forest Service finally accepted his recommendation, and so designated the Gila—40 years before the Wilderness Act.

AFTER SOME DISAPPOINTING YEARS with the Forest Service's Forest Products Laboratory in Madison, Leopold set out across the upper Midwest to survey the condition of wildlife. With a wife, five children, and little means of support, Aldo might have returned to Burlington and the Leopold Desk Company, but he had neither interest in nor aptitude for business.

For the American Game Conference, he helped write this country's first game policy, and he was appointed to President Franklin D. Roosevelt's Committee on Wildlife Restoration. In 1933 Charles Scribner's Sons published Leopold's *Game Management.*

*We of the industrial age boast of our control over nature. . . . there is no force in earth or sky which we will not shortly harness to build "the good life" for ourselves. But what is the good life? . . . We stand guard over works of art, but species representing the work of aeons are stolen from under our noses. . . . game can be restored by the creative use of the same tools which have heretofore destroyed it—axe, plow, cow, fire, and gun.*

Leopold had now defined a profession and written a classic, the foundation of the literature and still widely used today.

So impressed was the University of Wisconsin that it established for Leopold the country's first chair of game management. He taught an undergraduate course in wildlife ecology, but devoted most of his time to the few graduate students that he gathered around himself.

"A Ph.D. didn't impress him. His only concern was the quality of the individual."

"His concentration was intense. He'd get so wrapped up in what he was discussing that he'd forget to shift—kept his Chevrolet in second gear. Drove us crazy."

"He was always well dressed in the field, and around his neck hung that dog whistle and the Zeiss binoculars."

"He was a gentleman to the core."

"There was always a certain awe toward him, a distance between us. But there was a great feeling of respect."

"He was a man of enthusiasms, and in the field he really came alive. He was always growing intellectually."

"He was constantly pressing up to sharpen our powers of observation, of perception, always a gentle probing: 'I wonder why this field is abandoned?' "

In his essay "Natural History," Leopold held a typical zoology student up to the light:

*Instead of being taught to see his native countryside with appreciation and intelligence, he is taught to carve cats.*

A classroom exercise might be a deceptively simple landscape puzzle: a road flanked on one side by a subsiding telephone pole, then a pink granitic boulder, bluestem, oat stubble bearing ragweed, some young pine, poorer oat stubble; on the other side a *Silphium,* double-forked sumac, another pink rock, a fence post, and a bit of corn stubble. A rabbit lay dead on the road.

"How long ago was the last hard winter?" (Two years— the sumac's double fork.) "What sex is the rabbit?" (Male— females stay close to home in spring.) A final exam in wildlife management: "Select one plant or animal which you saw on the campus today and discuss its role in Wisconsin history."

"Dad could look at a piece of landscape and read its his-

tory from what he saw," his son Luna told me. "It's something he did better than anyone I know."

The Leopold home—modest, gray stucco—was only a mile from Aldo's office on campus. He walked to his office in early morning, strolled home for lunch and a short nap, returned and was back home around 5 p.m. He rarely brought work home; evenings were for the family.

"At dinner," Starker recalls, "Dad would pick one of us out and ask, 'What did you learn today?' Not what had you *done* that day but what you had *learned*—a big difference." There were three Leopold sons—Starker, Luna, and Carl—and two daughters, Nina and young Estella. "He was a wonderful father," Estella told me, "who had a brusque way about him. Whenever he came home, he'd get in his chair and be lost in his thoughts. But you felt comfortable."

"Mother followed the Spanish tradition of staying in the background," said Carl. "She absolutely adored Dad and never questioned him—ever. She viewed her place in life to keep a comfortable and happy home for him and us. She loved the shack, the plantings, the blooming of the wild flowers. These were all Dad's ideas, and she was really reveling in the things of Dad."

After dinner Aldo and Estella would sit together in the living room, often holding hands, listening to classical music or reading aloud from novels and plays.

His brother Frederic is convinced that Aldo could not have become what he became except for Estella. "She was completely selfless, though never made a show of it. She spoiled him—kept candy in his desk drawer—just as his mother had." To Estella fell the disciplining of the children.

In New Mexico, Aldo had carved and painted his own duck decoys from pine. Presents were not important to him unless handmade, so each Christmas the family made and exchanged gifts—a split-bamboo fly rod, a leather quiver. When the fireplace needed tools one Christmas, Luna and Starker bought a set from the store. Their father was unimpressed.

Soon after moving to Madison, Aldo was given a stave of yew. He carried it to the basement, and over the winter fashioned a bow. To make arrows, he sent off to Oregon for wands of Port Orford cedar. He used cow horn and deer antler for the nocks, shoemaker's thread for the bowstrings. "You do not annex a hobby," he wrote, "the hobby annexes you." The family entered archery tournaments shooting Leopold bows. Estella, much to her husband's delight, was the state women's champion for five years running.

But Leopold was to the core a hunter, and the kind of range that animated his nerve endings did not hold straw targets. With his brothers and sons, he returned for long hunting trips to the Gila and the Gavilán in Mexico. It was not the kill that mattered, but the hunt.

*Golf is a delightful accomplishment, but the love of hunting is almost a physiological characteristic. A man may not care for golf and still be human, but the man who does not like to see, hunt, photograph, or otherwise outwit birds or animals is hardly normal. He is supercivilized, and I for one do not know how to deal with him. Babes do not tremble when they are shown a golf ball, but I should not like to own the boy whose hair does not lift his hat when he sees his first deer.*

Hunting had always been Aldo's deep love, his excuse to be in the field and enjoy its subtle pleasures: handmade boots from Cutter's in Seattle, the balance of an Ainsley-Fox double-barrel, Gus freezing on point, a ruffed grouse exploding through the tamaracks, and at noon a pause to light a fire and sizzle a pork chop on a stick.

In Leopold's mind the virtue of hunting lay in the exercise of ethical restraints, dictated by the hunter's conscience, not by "a mob of onlookers."

For years Aldo had been looking for land near Madison to

use as a weekend retreat. On a bend of the Wisconsin River, he found an abandoned farm of marsh, a "corned-out" field, and a naked hill of drifting sand. The only standing structure was a chicken shed, its floor deep in manure. Leopold bought it.

THERE ARE TWO SPIRITUAL DANGERS *in not owning a farm. One is the danger of supposing that breakfast comes from the grocery, and the other that heat comes from the furnace. To avoid the first danger, one should plant a garden, preferably where there is no grocer to confuse the issue. To avoid the second, he should lay a split of good oak on the andirons, preferably where there is no furnace, and let it warm his shins while a February blizzard tosses the trees outside. If one has cut, split, hauled, and piled his own good oak, and let his mind work the while, he will remember much about where the heat comes from, and with a wealth of detail denied to those who spend the week end in town astride a radiator.*

The oak died one summer at the end of a bolt of lightning. After letting it "season for a year in the sun it could no longer use," the Leopolds laid a sharp saw to its trunk, while Estella, the "chief sawyer," cautioned against exhaustion. Years later Aldo reassembled "Good Oak" into rich metaphor.

*Fragrant little chips of history spewed from the saw cut . . . We sensed that these two piles of sawdust were something more than wood . . . that our saw was biting its way, stroke by stroke, decade by decade, into the chronology of a lifetime, written in concentric annual rings of good oak. . . .*

*Abruptly we began to cut the years of our predecessor the bootlegger, who hated this farm, skinned it of residual fertility, burned its farmhouse, threw it back into the lap of the County (with delinquent taxes to boot), and then disappeared among the landless anonymities of the Great Depression. . . . Rest! cries the chief sawyer, and we pause for breath.*

Aldo had always wanted to own land, to study and enrich

it. Almost immediately after buying the shack, the Leopolds planted Sudan grass, sorghum, and millet for wintering bobwhites and pheasants. They shoveled the manure out of the shack, laid a clay floor, and built a fireplace.

*Now our saw bites into the 1920's, the Babbittian decade when everything grew bigger and better in heedlessness and arrogance—until 1929, when stock markets crumbled. If the oak heard them fall, its wood gives no sign. . . . Rest! cries the chief sawyer, and we pause for breath.*

The following April, 2,000 red and white pine seedlings arrived on a truck. The Leopolds planted them all by hand.

*Now the saw bites into 1910-20, the decade of the drainage dream, when steam shovels sucked dry the marshes of central Wisconsin to make farms, and made ash-heaps instead. . . . Rest! cries the chief sawyer, and we pause for breath.*

Summer drought killed almost all the seedlings. In the cold mud of spring, the family planted more pine, and tamarack, wahoo, dogwood, hazel, white birch, hard maple. Another summer, another drought. They sharpened the shovels. More pine.

"Dad loved his tools," Carl Leopold recalls. "He had great scorn for anyone who had a dull shovel. He sharpened everything." Over the years, on their knees, the Leopolds would anchor their farm with some 36,000 pines.

*We cut 1905 when a great flight of goshawks came out of the North and ate up the local grouse (they no doubt perched in this tree to eat some of mine). . . . Rest! cries the chief sawyer, and we pause for breath.*

On Friday afternoons in Madison, while Estella collected the children and packed food for the shack, Aldo would sit quietly in the car with the engine running, itching to get going.

Aldo insisted that life at the shack remain simple, but bowing to Estella he bought lumber for a floor. Everything else

was made by hand, or scrounged. The river cast up bridge timbers. Made fine benches. They plucked a small table from the
Madison dump. The bunk springs were snow fences, the mat-
tresses of canvas and hay. In summer Aldo cooked outside over
an open fire, in winter in the fireplace; he was an artist with
the Dutch oven.

*Now our saw bites the 1870's, the decade of Wisconsin's
carousal in wheat. . . . I suspect that . . . the sand blow just
north of my oak had its origin in over-wheating. . . . Rest!
cries the chief sawyer, and we pause for breath.*

If history and the plow had denied him prairie, Aldo
would build his own. He made forays to unmowed cemeteries
and railroad embankments that still held the yellow splash of
*Silphium.* ("What a thousand acres of Silphiums looked like
when they tickled the bellies of the buffalo is a question never
again to be answered, and perhaps not even asked.") From
these remnants of prairie, he collected seeds of *Silphium*, cone-
flower, bluestem, wild rye, prairie dropseed. Near the shack he
stripped away the sod and dropped them in.

*The saw now severs 1865, the pith-year of our oak. In that
year John Muir offered to buy from his brother, who then
owned the home farm thirty miles east of my oak, a sanctuary
for the wildflowers that had gladdened his youth. His brother
declined to part with the land, but he could not suppress the
idea: 1865 still stands in Wisconsin history as the birth-year of
mercy for things natural, wild, and free.*

Recently, I visited the shack with Nina. Her mother had
died a few years before, and her brothers and sister had long
since scattered: Starker, once the prodigal, now retired as professor of wildlife and forestry at Berkeley; Luna, the hydrolo-
gist, who lives up the hill from Starker and who helped estab-
lish why rivers meander; Estella, a palynologist, now director
of the Quaternary Research Center in Seattle (all three are
members of the National Academy of Sciences); Carl, at Cor-
nell, a noted plant physiologist, polished, private, a fine classi-

cal guitarist. And Nina, who did not pursue a Ph.D. but is steeped in natural science. Aldo was careful not to push his children in any particular direction, but if they did something that pleased him, he showed it. "Isn't it interesting," said Carl, "how each of us may have gone into science partly to please Dad."

Nina and her husband live on what is now the Leopold Memorial Reserve: the family farm, bordered by a thousand acres that the neighboring farmers have covenanted to protect as wildlife habitat. The pines are now so thick they must be thinned; Nina's log home was built with Leopold pine.

Nina and I entered the shack. In a corner sat the canvas chair Aldo had made. Above the window hung Carl's toasting-fork spear (he used it to pluck carp from the flooded fields and plant them among the potatoes). I noticed deep cuts in the cedar log that Luna had emplaced as a mantel. In 1939 boys vandalized the shack, taking an ax to the mantel, puncturing pots and smashing plates. They poured kerosene in Estella's tins of homemade blackberry jam and wild honey. They stole Aldo's tools, and reduced his liquor supply.

"When we came in," Nina said, "all of us just went to a corner and began to cry. All, that is, but Dad. He just looked around, saw our state, and burst into a big smile. 'I didn't know how much this place meant to you,' he said. 'Let's get busy.' At night we would end up around the fireplace with guitars, singing. But Dad always went to bed early. We would ask what he wanted to hear. He would raise his head and say 'How about Brahms's "Lullaby"?' "

*Getting up too early is a vice habitual in horned owls, stars, geese and freight trains. Some hunters acquire it from geese, and some coffee pots from hunters. It is strange that of all the multitude of creatures who must rise in the morning at some time, only these few should have discovered the most pleasant and least useful time for doing it.*

Aldo Leopold was up well in advance of the birds. Around

3:30 or 4 a.m. the door of the shack would swing open, and Aldo would step out, a cup in his shirt, coffeepot in one hand, tiny notebook in the other. He would sit on the bench, have a sip, and listen. He also carried a light meter, and with each call would jot down bird, time, and footcandle: Song Sparrow, 4:32, -0.012.

*One hundred and twenty acres, according to the County Clerk, is the extent of my worldly domain. But the County Clerk is a sleepy fellow . . . at daybreak I am the sole owner of all the acres I can walk over. It is not only the boundaries that disappear, but also the thought of being bounded.*

Leopold believed that the future of American wildlife lay largely on private land, in the attitudes and decisions—wise or otherwise—of American farmers, not in the tape of bureaucracy. "At what point," he asked, "will governmental conservation, like the mastodon, become handicapped by its own dimensions?"

He likened his fellow conservationists to his bird dog Gus, who, when he couldn't find pheasants, pointed meadowlarks.

*This whipped-up zeal for unsatisfactory substitutes masked his failure to find the real thing. . . . We conservationists are like that . . . we have found us a meadowlark . . . the idea that if the private landowner won't practice conservation, let's build a bureau to do it for him.*

Leopold had always been somewhat of a loner, and he paid a price. At wildlife conferences, in articles, by force of his intellect, Aldo Leopold commanded the stage, but some in the wings were chilled in his shadow. He was not one of the boys.

In the 1940s Leopold saw that Wisconsin's irrupting deer herd was destroying the forests. Leopold was a member of the Conservation Commission. Trim the entire herd, not just bucks, he argued, or we will lose the deer and the woods for decades to come. He was called a Bambi killer.

"He wasn't naive," Starker told me, "but he believed in an

honest, straightforward presentation of the facts and debate. He was not a subtle politician. He became increasingly discouraged by the inability of the public to accept facts and by their propensity to get emotional."

Aldo's family saw a change come over him. At the shack he was still full of enthusiasm, but in Madison he withdrew more into troubled thought. He developed tic douloureux, a painful inflammation of the facial nerves that eventually required surgery at the Mayo Clinic. Sleep became more difficult, and he rose even earlier. Dawn would find him at his walnut desk at the office, well into another essay.

ON EXAMS, LEOPOLD WROTE: "Please boil down your writing; it will be graded for conciseness of expression." A student's paper on deer browse stated:

"The scope of this paper has been purposely limited to woody species common to the bear-oak type as it seemed desireable to lay particular emphasis upon the winter season when woody species were not only heavily utilized in general as browse but were even the sole food of deer following heavy snows."

Leopold concluded that meant: "We studied woody plants because deer depend on them in winter, and during snow, may eat nothing else."

Other great minds have died unexpressed. Leopold's ideas have survived because he was determined to master the craft of good writing, to wring of himself only the essence. He labored over his writing in pursuit of the fit word. He wrote on a yellow pad with a sharp pencil, his handwriting tiny and orderly, disguising the ferment in his mind. He would complete a paragraph, strike a vagueness, move a sentence around, light his pipe, pause in thought, then yelp as the flame reached his fingers.

The sun came up, his secretary came in. He kept writing,

cutting, simplifying. Still unsatisfied, he would put the piece away in the desk, his "cooler." A week, maybe months, later, after it had properly aged, he would pull it out and rework it more.

He was his own severest critic. After his death in 1948, the essay "Blue River" was found in his desk. It was but 14 sentences, a vivid, understated reflection on life and death—a cow, some green flies, the sudden arrival and departure of an ecstatic vermillion flycatcher: *the old cow was dead. . . . She had craned her neck—the mark was there in the sand—as if for one last look up into the cruel cliffs of Blue River.* Aldo had written a note on it to his wife: "Stella—do you think this is any good? It happened last year on the Blue. I've been thinking for a year how to write it. Afraid it can't be done." The note was dated June 11, 1922.

THERE ARE NO MONUMENTS to Aldo Leopold, save for a bronze plaque in the Gila. Just as well. Monuments were not his style. What mattered was that his ideas receive wider currency, but he died still in the minority and known only to a small audience. *A Sand County Almanac* was published posthumously and had only modest sales, until two decades later when the environmental movement discovered him.

What Leopold said of American conservation could be said of it today: We are too enamored of "show pieces. We have not yet learned to think in terms of small cogs and wheels" that determine healthy land. Only knowledge of its cogs and wheels can build a lasting affection for the land—and affection underpins ethics.

*We shall never achieve harmony with land, any more than we shall achieve justice or liberty for people. In these higher aspirations the important thing is not to achieve, but to strive. . . .*

In the past ten years we have created numerous environmental laws and institutions of government and cleaned up some polluted lakes and streams. But our striving suggests that as in Leopold's time we seem to be good for a few years of righteous flexing, yet lack endurance. Our patience is short and our self-interest deep. Lately our attention has drifted to the price of fuel, the shrinking dollar, the rumble of thunder from that part of the world on which we increasingly depend for a drive in the country. So we bend to digging up the West and probing the continental shelf for solutions. Confused and angered, we may look upon environmental laws, rather than our appetites, as the source of our current discontent. What was gained by one alarm may be lost by another.

Minds addicted to economics dismiss Leopold's land ethic as hopelessly idealistic. It is an ideal, but is it hopeless? Ethics guide, admittedly imperfectly, our relationships with one another. Can we not apply human values to the land? Leopold admitted that economic feasibility limits "the tether of what can and cannot be done for land. . . . The fallacy . . . is the belief that economics determines *all* land-use." Something more profound is at work. The farmer who refuses to plow to the road edge or drain the marsh because he will miss the quail and the crane knows this. And so, in his own way, does the city boy, who one evening sees the crane in flight, and feels his neck prickle.

Aldo Leopold observed that *recreational development is a job not of building roads into lovely country, but of building receptivity into the still unlovely human mind.*

*. . . all history consists of successive excursions from a single starting-point, to which man returns again and again to organize yet another search for a durable scale of values.* §

# A Listening Walk

*Gene Hill*

I THINK, now, that the thing my father liked best about bird hunting was the listening. The sounds you made through the crisp orange of the covers, so sharply punctuated by the abrupt quiet when you stopped. The straining to hear the tinkling of the dog bell, the sorting out of all the little noises until what you wished for came through the rest. Past the rustling of the trees, under the wind, over and around the calling of the crows and the barking of distant farm dogs, the threadlike tingle of the little 5-cent bell would call us off to some new and exciting direction.

Now and then we'd stop, trying to catch the waxing and waning, trading disappointment for eagerness, the bafflement of silence leaving the next steps to our woodsmen's judgment until one of us could see the dog standing there on point, her head turned to our footsteps until she was sure we'd seen her. One off to each side we walked, and then, at the sound of the shot, we'd stand dead still, putting the rolling boom away in our memory against the instant silence that suddenly seemed almost a rebuke to the violent sound of the shot. Sometimes one of us would speak, sometimes not. The ritual then was not to talk just for the sake of talking. Idle chatter wasn't the way of country people. We were as thrifty with our emotions as we were with our little money. Chattering was looked on as impolite or worse, emptyheadedness. Bird hunting was a private delight.

The woods are where I go when I'm starved for quiet. But, of course, the quiet is only relative. Few things in nature have idle tongues. The chattering of a squirrel will alert those of its kind that are listening—as it's meant to do. The scolding of the jay precedes my presence like a siren. These are important sounds to creatures that live by listening. As a small boy I used to practice walking, as careful as a warring Iroquois not to snap a twig or rattle a rock, and few things filled me with more pride than to walk up on a browsing deer and be able to stand so still that I could pass for a tow-headed, slightly ragged, runny-nosed tree. And I still take a certain amount of joy in my quiet ways, helped along by some dulling deafness, absorbing the small, now-and-then bits and pieces of quiet like a tonic. I take to the woods alone a lot more than I used to in younger days.

You stand there and the scratching of a match to light your pipe sounds like a tearing of canvas. But you don't dare stand still too long or the silence forbids the idea of moving. You begin, after a while, to shed a few of the layers of man and you understand, however so insignificantly, the demand for quiet that is instinctive in an animal in the wild—the ghost fears that have existed for a hundred thousand years.

So we follow the old dog, shuffling along well inside the need for a whistle, knowing that any chance for a bird is slim and knowing that's not really why we are here. We are not really here to shoot birds this time. We are after something else. We are looking for that layer inside us, that subconscious antenna, that feeling that here, in these woods, we are washing something away in the quiet.

We come to watch the beaver and understand his hurry to get things done. We note the rubbings of the buck and the heavy nests of the squirrels. Most of the songbirds have left, and you stop and imagine, or try to, that the lady jay is two thousand miles away and in four or five months will find her way back to just where her bold and cheeky mate is perched, telling you that you haven't spoofed him for a minute. Some crows are worrying an unseen owl who couldn't care less. The old dog comes back and asks us a question, and to humor her sense of industry we move on.

They ask me, "What do you think about in the woods?" I tell them all sorts of things, but actually I'm trying not to think of anything special at all. This is the country of few second chances for the unwary, and you might think about that. Or you might wonder about the certain odd shape of a stone and turn it over with your foot and think about it trying that side up for another few hundred years. Just idle ruminations of the mind. Animal curiosity.

My father especially liked the sound of snow falling. He used to say "listen . . . ," and I couldn't hear anything but the softness. It took me years to understand what he heard in the sounds of snow and rain and that it was possible to understand something and never be able to explain it—that some sounds you absorbed deeper than in the labyrinths of the ear. What does the bark of a fox sound like to the mouse? Or the croak of the heron to the frog? I tell the old dog that none of these are the voices of poets and she, to humor me, agrees.

The work shift changes with the coming of twilight and the voices wane. There is a chorus of good nights as the pheasants pull the covers up over their heads. The fox barks to let them know he is there, but I think they know already. If you're a pheasant, the fox is always there. An owl orders silence and gets it. Some odd night birds call, forever mysteries to me; others have voices I can put faces on. The old dog has heard the pheasants too and looks over her shoulder to see if I'm following. I am, but unwillingly. Ordinarily I leave the roosting covers alone in my theory that a man's house is his castle and that goes for the pheasants as well, but the old dog is sort of twisting my arm and reminding me that there is some time to go before dark. I try to argue with her but it's no use. She reminds me that we took a bird or two there when she was a puppy and I tell her that was training and she says that she's old and can't see or hear too well anymore and has to make do. We head toward the little swamp, she at a trot, looking back to make sure I'm there.

The quiet is palpable now. All I can hear is the dog splashing back with the cock bird. I turn away and head back toward the car and she follows along with her prize.

I feel guilty at having broken a promise I long ago made to myself. But I have given the old dog her way and now it's too late for remorse. How often we have to reflect on the price of satisfaction—the toss of a coin, so to speak, that often seems as willful and arbitrary as the Roman judges in the Coliseum.

I take the bird and carry it myself, and I can hear the delighted snuffling of the old dog as she shuffles along, poking her nose into the feathers to reassure herself that the bird is still there. We stop and take a last minute to look at the ruby eyebrow of the setting sun and listen to nothing. I unload the gun and slip the shells into my pocket. What I want, right now, is to hear another cock bird calling from the swamp, a voice that will echo through the evening mist with a wild bravado to reassure me that this little corner of my world is still quick with life. I know it is, for we heard half a dozen crowings just before the old dog had her way, and I want someone to tell me now that the incident has already been forgotten. But nothing happens.

I, who had wanted only a quiet walk, have become the owl *and* the fox. I, who had gone only to listen, have become the one who was listened to.

Sitting by the car I dress and pick the pheasant. The old dog stretches herself out for a little nap and the feathers drift over her dull, black coat. I take a handful and slide them under her nose and she thumps her tail without opening her eyes. I think that I ought to tell her the story of Eden, but being a woman, I'm sure she understands it far better than I do. I tell her that I'm just a pushover for a pretty face, but she knows that too. She climbs into the front seat with me, ignoring her kennel in the back, puts her head on my lap, and sleeps. §

# The Everyday Letort

*Harrison O'Connor*

O BSERVE THE USUAL feeding behavior; the long, staring pause before the convulsive, lurching gulp and an-
gry chomping of jaws and spitting up of gelatinous algae.
Presented with an unusual food item, they feel the nervous
energy of indecision. One cannot but notice the irritability ex-
pressed by the ticking motion of the head. "Should I? No, no!"
is clearly spoken by those mute lips. Their initiative so often
punished, they fret decisions; taught by fear, they adhere to a
regimen. When not withdrawn to dark rooms, they may wan-
der up at any hour to appease appetites dulled but comforted
by a repetitious diet. "A cress bug is a cress bug," say the grim
brown trout of Pennsylvania's Letort Creek.

I fish the Letort 20 weekends a year. Every month of the
calendar, knee-deep in muck or in snow, I stalk these coffee-
and-cream-colored browns. Not every newcomer finds the Letort exciting to the eye, however. I have been told, somewhat
huffily, that "I like to fish under the hemlocks," and I have

wanted to reply, "I don't fish for scenery." That is not true, though. From the first day I have loved the derelict appearance of this spring run.

I was initially struck by the dark, secretive pulsing of the limestone-green flow, not realizing that the mysterious appearance was a lack of reflected light off a gravel bottom. There is no gravel, not even where a chute cuts deeply through the many feet of muck that years of weed growth and subsequent siltation have accumulated. I yanked up handfuls of cress and immediately felt the skin-crawling presence of hundreds of sow bugs and shrimp. I stooped my head low over shallow water and saw a scudopolis: Every inch of bottom was alive with the slow motion of cress bugs. Then I went looking for the rising trout for which the Letort is famous.

One walks through swampy meadows, through pasture luxuriant if rank with weed, through long, tree-darkened stretches of stream, all the while listening to the roar of an interstate highway, the sirens of a fire department, the takeoffs and landings of small aircraft, the buzzing of lawnmowers, the voices of neighbors calling over fences, and the sudden roar of approval from a nearby baseball park.

Unmoved by the clamor, the eye sees only the utterly calm and silently flowing spring water and, now and again, a trout. The fishing is seldom good enough to become all-encompassing, but the remarkable stealth of the trout insists that the eye remain sharp. This trespassing into the business of trout through the backyards of men makes me feel like a ghost. Clear-headed, smoothly flowing, exactly on edge between two species, I am neither reminded of responsibility (unless a small child cries when I suddenly feel dreary) nor committed to action. Instead, I am poised. Poised for hours, a wonderful state of mind.

Since regulations permit the killing of one trophy fish over 20 inches, one easily becomes obsessed with wanting to see such a fish. I supposed daybreak to be my best chance.

Many has been the dawn when I arrived to see every trout in the stream, or so it seemed, actively rooting, their tails flapping in the air as they darted forward to gulp a shrimp, a feeding tempo as regular as a rise to a good hatch. Relaxed by the night, the fish had worked themselves up to this accelerated feeding. The tempo of their tailing was the measure of their confidence. The fisherman hopes to match the rhythm of his casting to the fish's impulse to feed. The faster the trout tails, the easier it is to slip him a fraud.

Those mornings taught me where to look when the stream appears dead, as it usually does. The rooters—trout ranging in size from 13 to 16 inches, with a few up to 18 inches long—rise up out of the green holes, slither across the water-skimmed banks of mud and submerged cress, and make their way into narrow, silt-bottomed sloughs between the cress beds or between the cress and the grassy bank, wherever little current flows.

If I positioned myself to polarize the glare on the water, I could see trout hovering in inches of water in these alleys. They seemed in a stupor, barely finning in the slack current, but occasionally one tipped down and scooped a scud off bottom, the tail barely wrinkling the surface, the mouth flashing white.

I cannot say how many days I walked along the Letort looking for rising trout, all the way presented with the challenge of rooting trout. Seldom did I meet another fisherman, although just a few miles away there are limestone streams so flogged by flyfishermen that the trout tolerate anglers rollcasting line across their backs. I finally asked myself, can it be that the Letort, inspiration for *The Modern Dry Fly Code, In the Ring of the Rise* and *Rising Trout,* hosts a population of brown trout that prefer rooting to rising? Had I thought more carefully about the stream's apparent lack of popularity, I should have guessed that the Letort does not offer the predictable hatch action that most flyfishermen seek. One expert trout fisherman

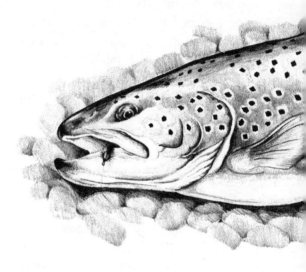

told me the Letort was finished. Yet my eyes saw that the stream was overloaded with constantly feeding, one-and-a-half-pound trout. It is the tempo and style of the feeding that has turned everyone off.

From time to time during the heat of the day, I did see midstream rise forms. But experience taught me that these free risers, usually holding in the main current at the tail end of the holes, are nearly always trout under 12 inches in length. The bigger fish, when they rise, need to feel disguised. They typically choose stations out of the current, under an overhanging tussock of grass or beneath a low bridge.

On the Letort, the size of the fish governs its feeding habits in this way: the "yearlings" rush here and there in the pools and show a preference for food on the surface; but once a trout grows to 13 inches, he chooses a much more energy-efficient feeding station in the shallows. But so extremely self-conscious does he feel, holding in half a foot of water, and so

vulnerable, having wiggled across broad mud banks to a position many feet away from his hiding hole, that he depends for his safety upon minimal movement. Though grasshoppers sail in the meadows and beetles hang in the bushes and the yearlings blip-blip in the pools, most days he deliberately roots scuds. Those trout able to grow over 18 inches long at this point quit the shallows, at least during the day. They are large enough to feed on the ample supply of crawfish that begin to move with darkness.

Observe the typical Letort trout, a fat 15-incher. When he first arrives on station, at the tail end of a shallow trough of slow water, he does not move at all for quite some time. Barely finning, he seems to stare straight ahead. Like a groundhog that first rears to scan a memorized view before feeding, this trout watches his limited horizon for movement.

At last he carefully tips down and scoops up a cress bug, an action as subtle as a quick discard from an expressionless card player. So begins the listless tailing that does not mark the surface except for the occasional wrinkle. The fish is well aware that eagerness gives away his game.

After a period of successful, unmolested feeding, he begins to work a beat. Now the trout darts forward two feet to intercept a shrimp—no cress bug requires such effort. Chomping his mouth, settling back away from the puff of disturbed mud, he watches the edge of the cress for another victim, then darts forward again, and so progresses up the alley.

Finally he turns, swims back to the beginning of the beat, and after another period of watchful waiting, resumes the patrol. That his tail now regularly breaks the surface at the moment of interception indicates the fish has slightly relaxed, though certainly the tempo of the tailing is not as accelerated as during the dawn sprees. By bright of day the trout keeps up his guard with intervals of watchful immobility, a habit that is rewarded when unobservant anglers walk by on the banks; for the more times the fish routinely scoots to the safety of his green hole, the surer of his shallow feeding station he becomes.

The really good rooting trout, one that's 17 or 18 inches long, tails at a rate that is less regular and even-spaced. Halfway up the beat, he turns and scoots out into the pool, reappears one minute later at the starting position, picks up one or two cress bugs, then swims up the alley and enters a pocket of backwater, there to linger and stare. This whimsical pattern, rooting interrupted with scoots of nervous swimming, suggests the trout knows that the more unpredictably he feeds, the less vulnerable he is to being tricked by a properly pitched fly.

Later, during the terrestrial part of the day, the occasionally grubbing trout is observed ticking with nervous hesitation and excitement when a wriggling ant passes overhead. How he relishes the sharp taste of ant! But after hours of disciplined tailing, how loath he feels to make a move so bold as a rise, an action that recalls the hook's sting from yearling days.

Eventually, the trout does rise. He completes the action with an alarmed scoot forward, just as if he had felt the hook, a nervous response telling of the fish's experience. Then he settles into a pattern of rooting interspersed with a few daring rises. I have hidden in the bushes and watched a trout gulp down a couple of cress bugs almost angrily, then rise carefully for a floating insect, then root again.

It has been my observation that such a trout, when presented with a floating artificial, is far more selective—concentrating his mental energies on making the decision to rise—than when he is offered a sinking fly that reaches his depth. The opposite should be true—in the slow current, the fish can take a better look at the wet fly. Yet I have taken Letort browns with pink maggots, nothing more than a wide-gapped hook wrapped in pink floss ribbed with copper wire, a quick-sinking fly that cannot resemble either a cress bug or a shrimp. I believe the fly simply slipped up on the trout, triggering the go-ahead response from a fish that has spent hours maintaining his invisibility by careful rooting. The floating artificial excites him, concentrates his mental powers; but it asks him to break out of that comforting groove of rooting, which lets the trout feel most secure since the cress bugs are always there. The sunken fly asks only that he open his mouth.

It's possible that this same trout, with growing confidence, warming water temperature and an abundance of surface food, may slip into the groove of rising. If so, he is usually an easier fish to catch because he is so much more interested in the menu than the listless rooter. On those rare days when I have found the fish committed to surface feeding, I have had my best scores. But if something should frighten this rising fish, he will scoot for his dark hole; when he resumes feeding, he will again root up his confidence before rising.

The angler cannot always expect to find rising trout, even during the prime terrestrial hours of late season. Rather, he will encounter fish displaying varying degrees of self-confidence. That one over there, caught just this morning, fins sullenly. Another has chosen a feeding station where he is regularly flushed by passing anglers, or even couples out for a walk along the railroad tracks. Out of nervous habit, he tails, scoots out into the pool, then returns to root again. A third trout rises steadily in the middle of a brushpile where the angler's fly rarely interrupts his concentration on choice food.

The Letort fisherman must observe each trout, not merely to see whether he is rising or rooting, but to determine at which tempo, and how voraciously. Then match the hatch if you will but, more important, match the mood. The choice of fly is more psychological than entomological. For instance:

On the inside bank of a bend in the stream, a gentle rise form disturbs the slack water—a welcome sight for the fisherman frustrated by a morning of rooters. I move into position where I can watch the fish. Ah, the trout dips forward, tail barely wrinkling the surface. Moments later, something passes over his head and the fish twitches. Does he want to rise? Is he afraid to rise? He is not tailing vigorously, not in that groove of rooting. Apparently he hasn't been feeding steadily on terrestrials either; he clearly lacks confidence. He looks like a trout in a "normal" stream that is waiting for a hatch. I believe this fish is waiting on his nerve.

At last he eases up and sips something off the surface. Then he roots, once, twice. I see all the signs of caution in a fish that has not been at his station for a long time. Because of his reluctance to show himself, I choose not to offer a dry fly. I ponder my flybox.

If I select a wet fly tied on a No. 24 to No. 28 hook—say a floating mayfly nymph or midge pupa—I won't have the necessary sink rate and the trout must still rise. A fly as large as a No. 16 could easily frighten this fish, he that fins suspiciously in the slackest of currents. Why not make the obvious choice and pitch him a small cress bug? Instead, my fingers pinch a No. 20 lacquered black ant out of the box. This fly will sink quickly and may stimulate the fish to move for his food. To interest a fish in a cress bug, the presentation must be perfect. But for an ant, the trout perhaps will move a foot. The sinking ant tempts him with, "Here's one you don't have to rise for."

I have since had my good dry fly days: "June 4—sulphur action"; "August 21—unbelievable heat and humidity, with the fish picking up terrestrials all afternoon"; "October 7—a sudden flying ant hatch." Such days are rare. So is the morning when you arrive expecting to stalk rooters, immediately see a rise form, and say to yourself, "*Now* the floating ant will do its work." Uncommon are those dawn sprees when every fish in the stream is tailing, not merely greedily, but euphorically (though mornings in May are a good time to anticipate such action, which will last until 11:00 a.m.). And if you fish the stream persistently, you will discover the free-rising, mature trout of late season that has made the Letort famous—this trout, having found a station that is either inaccessible to most angling or so hidden from the angler's eye, has developed the confidence to think only about preferred food. But it is the rooting trout on which the Letort fisherman must depend for day-in, day-out sport. It has always been that way.

Any organized description by me on how to catch these rooters would be a lie. In fact, I am still working on the basic pieces of the puzzle. I can say this, however: Of any spring creek I have fished, the Letort offers the finest finishing course on the problems of approaching skittery trout.

Lying in bathtub-sized puddles of open water in the cress, able to feed merely by tipping forward, these trout concentrate their full attention on the fisherman. They come to depend upon his habit of wearing bright clothes, of following paths beside the stream, of moving steadily, of casting repetitiously, and of preferring certain flies. I have a friend who liked to wear a dapper, white fishing vest. How the stream punished him!

My biggest mistake may be that I like to creep close to a trout to see every flicker of fin. I often take one step too many. Perhaps, unconsciously, I recall those days when a fine rain, not really a rain at all, pinpricks the surface, when a fisherman can almost walk the fly into the mouth of an unsuspecting fish. The close-stalking game seems to depend upon the lighting. Certainly the fish are more relaxed on overcast days, feed more regularly, and therefore are more easily caught. Yet there is a particularly penetrating brightness under a certain dark sky that, though it gives excellent visibility to the angler, also allows the trout to see backwards an extra 15 feet.

Most of the rooters I have caught were taken from the near bank, where I was able to stalk within 40 feet. Total passivity is the sign of a wary fish. By crouching close behind such a fish, within "pitching range," I can choose the best moment to cast, just when the trout lets down his guard and activates his hunting instincts. My first throw is usually off. Or else the fish tails just as I start casting. In either case, I wait until the fish is again preoccupied before I lift my line off the water—an action that frequently disturbs the cress, signaling the alert trout to freeze up and wait for further evidence.

At this close range, one can actually sense the fish's mood in order to know how long to wait before casting again. If the trout's head turns toward the fly, then back, then toward the fly again, in slight but sudden movements—he seems to be ticking with indecision—then the fly is right or nearly so; but for the moment, for reasons of drag or something else, it is wrong. If the same fly is immediately pitched back above the aroused fish, even if the throw is drag-free and on target, the trout will not budge. Once disturbed by doubt, these fish habitually settle into a well-rehearsed groove of slow-finning, watchful passivity.

If a too-eager fisherman persists by casting, the fish will simply stare at the fly, and stare, and stare, though each presentation swims the fly within inches of his snout. Finally, the trout will unlock his hold in the feeble current and begin drifting. Ever so deliberately, he will back down the alley, then suddenly turn and scoot out into the deep (all this only if the presentation is not frightening, for any big mistake on the part of the angler immediately results in a scooting fish). Now, whenever I see that fixed, bug-eyed staring at a fly, or notice a fish drift tentatively backwards, I rest the trout for a good ten minutes.

When a Letort brown likes a floating fly, he quivers with excitement. A good sunken fly he simply gulps. I believe a fly-tier has to exercise more skill dressing a floater than a sinker. As to what makes a good fly for this stream, the obvious answer is one that is black. The starling-hackled midge, the ant, the cricket and the sculpin, all tied in black, are a range of flies that will move these browns. Productive dry flies are: a No. 24 Adams, a No. 24 black Humpy, a No. 16 house fly, a No. 16 black ant and a No. 24 flying ant. Actually, an angler fishing the Letort in September and October could also do well with odd, low-profile dries that float in the film.

Most days, however, the choice of flies is all too simple: a small fly that sinks promptly. A cress bug, a black, lacquered ant, the same sinking ant with a red floss tail, a maggot tied with black, white or pink floss, a fat hare's ear, a fore-and-aft hackled peacock, in fact any quick-sinking buggy fly will catch rooters. I have not found a good shrimp pattern.

The ploppy sound of a chunky No. 20 wet fly must ring a familiar bell with these fish. Time and time again I have made a poor cast, plopping such a fly to the side and behind a fish, only to see him turn promptly and sometimes take. Though he is rooting, he hears the terrestrial plop, turns involuntarily, sees a fly sinking at a natural speed, and takes because he does not have to think about rising.

When casting to a tailing fish, I sometimes can see the sunken, drifting fly—that is how close this game may be played. If I cannot see the fly, I watch for any sudden movement of the trout's head in order to know when to strike. Now and again I make a perfect cast and the fly floats right into the fish's mouth. I see that suddenly irritable headshaking, the gill flaps fluttering as the trout tries to rid himself of the sticky, offset hook. I lift deliberately to feel him. So light is the strike that the fish is not certain what has happened—feeling no resistance (I instantly drop the rod tip to horizontal), he does not boil away for the deep, but scoots forward two feet, then fins nervously, waiting and watching. The fish is hooked and he doesn't even know the battle has begun. Rod pointed straight at the fish, I reel up the extra flyline, then lift to start that panicked, swooshing scoot for the deep hole. For me, that is *the* moment in fishing, not the landing of a played-out fish. §

# Old Friend Now Departed

*Pete Kaminsky*

L AST APRIL, two weeks into the season, I lost my fishing partner, Gene. Gene was an illustrator who worked for the agency that did Ford ads. He was good at it, but he really didn't give a tinker's damn for Madison Avenue. He worked so he could fish and he fished all the time, breaking his routine to tie flies, mostly nymphs. Gene had forsworn the dry fly. "Trout eat nymphs more than they eat duns," he used to say. Gene's ambition was to work out a series of nymphs for the Esopus Creek, one of trout fishing's hallowed streams—cutting, tumbling, falling and pooling through 16 miles of Catskill greenery. Together we fished behind every rock in it.

Like the artist, John Atherton, who wrote *The Fly and the Fish,* Gene applied the principles of painting and color and form to his flies. His bible was Ernest Schweibert's *Nymphs.* But it was, to Gene, a flawed scripture. "That goddamn Schweibert doesn't know what the hell he's talking about," Gene would remark and then set about tying a better fly (sometimes it really was better). At the end of last season he had told me that he was ready for dry flies again. He thought he'd done what he'd set out to do. Next year, he and I were going to tear them up.

And then he died. I found out when I called his office. "Is Gene there?" I said.

"Hold on," they said. Someone put a hand over the phone and I heard muffled conversation.

A woman picked up the phone. "Were you a friend of Gene's?" she asked. That was all she needed to say.

I wondered if maybe Gino had seen the damage done by the April floods when, in the space of three hours, nine inches of rain had fallen on the unthawed ground. If you loved that stream as he did, it would have been your undoing too. I can still see large trout floating in the aisles of our supermarket— wild rainbows, belly up between the Drano and the Froot Loops.

The river never did come back that year. The flood broke mountains, ripped trees from their roots and tossed house trailers about the way a bad drunk might upset things when he rises from the table. And every rain brought landslides that turned the river a dark and heartless red for weeks on end.

I guess the river was as pissed off about Gene as I was. Or maybe the river didn't care at all, but it sure acted as if it did.

Then Tony Atwill came down from Vermont to sample our Catskill waters, Tony having had his fill of uncatchable Battenkill trout. He pulled into the drive one fine morning, wadered, leadered and ready to go.

"What'll it be Atwill? Wanna fish for gypsy moths or dead mink?"

Tony caught my drift and agreed when I suggested that we'd do well to drive over the mountains to the valley of the Schoharie, which had been spared the full force of the flood.

So we drove, covering some 20 miles where the land

changes from rocky Catskill high plateau to more gentle, grousey-looking farm and forest. Art Flick's Schoharie. *Down by the banks of the mighty Schoharie,* I hummed to the tune of an old country song about love gone wrong. It was good to have a friend close by. The day, the company, and the fishing to come were truly a tonic to me, not so much the fountain of youth as a spring flowing up clear from the ground, tickling the moss and fallen leaves.

We passed the tavern, climbed the highway and reached the turn-off for the bridge.

Now I'm sure you know about bridges and streams and fishermen. First thing is, bridges are usually built over good fishing holes. Second thing is, kids jump off the ledges all day or swing out over the water, holding on to a long rope, letting go at the height of their swing, falling into the water, scaring the fish. Third thing is, in such places, which are easy to get to, the resident fish have seen everything thrown at them and then some. The smart angler knows better than to waste his time in such spots. The smart angler gets geared up and walks two miles through a swamp to get to the *real* fishing, dismissing the blackflies as a necessary but obnoxious rite of passage.

But, no matter how smart you are, you do stop by the bridge, as we did, and you do lean over the railing, shading your eyes from the sun. And you say, "There's one." And your friend says, "No, it's just a sucker." And you agree and the two of you go somewhere else.

*Except,* right then and there, at high noon under a hot summer sun, we saw the biggest trout of our lives. She rose up through 20 feet of water and ledges, finned for a second and inhaled a struggling caddis fly. Just as slowly she descended. We turned to one another, stared for a second and spoke, "Nah, it just couldn't be." We almost bumped heads as we leaned over for just one more look. Then, as if she knew her part in our little play, the trout stirred again, moving back to her home. I wear a 35-inch sleeve. She was as long as my arm.

Slapping our suspenders over our shoulders, wading in with shoes untied, we hit the stream, rods held in our teeth. We cast and cast and cast. Dries, wets, nymphs, streamers, cow dung and aspirin. We didn't catch a thing, of course. Six hours we fished for that brown.

We stopped at the tavern for a long-necked Bud. Long necks are hard to find these days, and that tavern is my end-of-the-day treat whenever I get up to the Schoharie.

Once home, we mixed a pitcher of Rob Roys, Gene's favorite drink, not the least of his contributions to my spiritual well-being. As we sank deep into our cups, Gene's widow rapped at the window. Gene would be with her, I thought. Gene with his ratty green sweater, his blue jeans and Civil War-issue moccasins. He would be carrying a pot full of trout in fiery-hot Fra Diavola sauce (Gene was New York Bronx to the core). The trout would be decent-sized with a few three-inchers thrown in because, flyfisherman though he was, he had a city kid's inability to throw away *any* food. Gene with his tight, curly hair turned snow-white from the cobalt treatments ten years past. The hair was a badge of survival to him. He'd beaten cancer and counted these last years as double-scale over-time.

She entered alone. In her hands a little box from Tiffany's such as might have held a ring at one time. There were two dry flies in the box, Gene's last. And there was one very big, very ugly stonefly—the kind hen browns like.

My wife saw the look in our eyes, knew she couldn't stop us and simply requested that we fasten our safety belts.

We left at midnight, driving like the wind, speakers blasting, foot to the floorboard, and any deer dumb enough to cross our path could go to the devil. We had a mission. The moon was already high in the sky; silver shadows of back-lit clouds covered the mountains as we retraced our way, back up past the tavern to the bridge.

As we drove, there was no question in our minds of hooking the trout. The scene was so right, so just, so complete to the last detail. We dwelt on the strategy of playing the fish. Perhaps it would be better to wade out onto the ledges so that the trout would make for the far shore, clear of obstacles.

Atwill, who has a sense of justice, offered to artillery-spot for me. He wrapped himself in an old blanket and took up his sentry post on the bridge. From below he looked like a not very prosperous Arab.

If I were the kind of man I'd like to be, I would have paused at that moment to commune with Gino. But I didn't. Couldn't have done it even if I tried. There was too much trout, too much aliveness, for any spirit to come between me and the fish.

I tried his fly. I fished it upstream and down. I tied it to a sinking line and repeated my tactics. It didn't work. I clipped it off and felt no guilt, which was good. I tried big bushy dries and lacy marabou matukas. I moved to the tail of the pool because I'd read all those stories that guarantee "Cannibal Browns Cruise the Shallows at Night"—but not those shallows, not that night.

Life, I reflected on the drive home, rarely rises to the level of Art.

But we keep trying. §

# Shorebird Hunting: The Way It Was

*Paul Rundell*

F EW PEOPLE ARE NOW ALIVE who remember it as it was. Today, the curious musical names—curlew, plover, yellow-legs, knot—are never mentioned by gamebird hunters. But once, when dense flocks of them darkened the beaches and prairies, these species and others were eagerly hunted for market and for sport. The shorebirds represent a near-forgotten chapter in American shooting history. Their story should be retold so that it may be preserved.

Some of the earliest published accounts of American hunting by men like Frank Forester, Elisha Lewis and William Elliott show that hunting for shorebirds and their upland cousins was already well established by the middle decades of the nineteenth century. Many species were thriving. Snipe, willet, sandpiper, plover, dowitcher, yellowlegs, curlew and rail could all be part of a day's bag in those times. Today, only snipe and rails remain for hunters. Most of the others had been taken off the hunting lists by the time of World War II.

The years between the Civil War and the beginning of the twentieth century were remarkable ones for American sportsmen. A growing firearms industry was turning its efforts to the development and production of breech-loading sporting guns. Game animals and gamebirds were plentiful and widespread. Hunting opportunities were so great that this period has been termed the Golden Age of American hunting. Nash Buckingham called these decades the "prodigal years"—a time when men hunted and shot with abandon. The wealth of game, particularly birds, seemed limitless.

The groupings of species loosely called shorebirds represented this abundance and variety of game. Rails (actually a member of a class called wading birds) were hunted from boats in tidal marshes in the East and South. On the sand flats and water-bordered meadows one could find curlew, willet, yellowlegs and other birds. Plover were hunted along the Atlantic Coast and as far inland as the prairies of the Midwest. The widely distributed snipe was hunted in low meadowlands and wet pastures throughout its range.

Since these species were migratory, the absence of game laws permitted both spring and fall hunting in many sections of the country. In the Midwest particularly, spring hunting for plover and curlew was done during the spring migration north to the birds' breeding grounds.

Golden, black-bellied and upland plover were abundant and eagerly sought by gunners. Unusual methods were developed to hunt these birds. Golden plover would respond to skillful whistling that mimicked their shrill cry. One way to hunt them was to burn off an area of old field or pasture before the flights began. The new grass that sprung up would attract the birds. A shallow pit was dug to accommodate one or two people. When the flights began, the gunner would spread his decoys, retire to his pit where his head might be camouflaged with a green cap, and wait for the birds to come. A skilled hunter would not shoot when the birds first swung by his decoys. Instead, he would try to fire when they were bunched at the right distance so that many birds might be killed with the first shot. Survivors might be whistled in again and again, so that three or four shots could be taken at one flock.

In the West during spring shooting, hunters after plover selected a spot on the birds' flight path. They lay on the ground while wearing neutral clothing for concealment. The plover often flew close to the ground, and a gunner frequently knocked down several birds from a closely bunched flock with his first shot.

When the birds were feeding on the bare ground or closely cropped pastures, it became difficult to approach the flocks or predict their flight patterns. Under such conditions, different tactics were required. A horse and buggy was often employed to allow the gunner to get close enough to the flock for a shot. Deception was the key here. Plover that would flush much too soon if a man walked toward them were more tolerant of a wagon. If the line of approach was not direct and the pace was brisk the birds would not take flight. The buggy was driven swiftly in a path that appeared to take it by the bunched birds, and as the distance between hunter and hunted shrunk the man had to gauge his chances carefully. At the right moment he stopped the horse and fired quickly, for the birds would flush. An experienced hunter might be able to shoot once into the packed flock on the ground and shoot again as they took flight.

Both golden plover and upland plover (a true sandpiper but similar to the plover in habitat and behavior) were hunted in this manner. Variations of buggy hunting were also practiced. The "stalking horse" tactic was frequently used. A hunter would walk next to the horse's shoulders on the side away from the birds. A gradual approach was employed, and at the right moment the hunter would halt and fire, after the horse or team had moved out of the way. The birds didn't seem to notice another pair of legs as the man walked on the other side of the horse. They would usually fly the moment the hunter showed himself, but sometimes additional advantage could be gained by walking quickly toward the flock. Quick and obedient horses were neded for either technique, and a steady animal little bothered by smoke and gunfire was a valuable asset.

Sometimes two men worked together, particularly when they were hunting the wary upland plover in autumn. One hunter would lie down or conceal himself in a selected spot after a flock was located, while the second would drive the wagon around the birds and approach them from the opposite side. He would take his shots and hope the flushed birds would pass over the concealed partner, who would also have opportunity to fire into the flock.

The plover were valued as table fare; well-fed birds were plump and delicious. As a consequence many were sold to the markets, where epicures prized them during the spring and summer months. As populations of other species such as the passenger pigeon dwindled late in the nineteenth century, market gunners turned their attention to plover. Many were shipped to the cities. As prices increased, more and more hunters met the migrations. According to some stories, refrigerator cars were sent to the hunting areas, where they were filled and shipped back to the Chicago markets.

The black-bellied plover gained a reputation as a fine gamebird. A swift, wary flier, this bird was difficult to shoot. Cape Cod gunners called black-bellied plover "beetleheads." They hunted them from stands built on the tidal meadows or on mud flats near feeding areas. Another method was to hunt them from pits dug in the high beaches where the birds roosted at high tide. The birds often returned to the same roosting areas again and again, and these spots could be located by the many tracks in the sand. It was necessary to finish the hole soon after the incoming tide began to cover the flats, for the birds

would soon be moving to the roosts. Old birds were particularly wary, and it was necessary to conceal any hole with boards and sand. Black-bellied plover were difficult to decoy and would seldom land to the decoys, especially if they were on the beaches. Elsewhere, if blinds were carefully made and very natural in appearance, and if the hunter could imitate the cry of the bird perfectly, he might have some shooting.

Curlews were slightly larger than plover and were occasionally found intermingled in the same flocks. At least three species were hunted: the long-billed, the Hudsonian and the Eskimo curlew. Long-billed and Eskimo curlews were widely distributed and eagerly hunted. They were large shorebirds, and their size and delicious flesh made them tempting quarry. The long-billed curlew could be decoyed and lured in by imitating its loud, musical whistle. The cries of a wounded curlew would attract other members of the flock which would circle overhead, permitting the gunner additional shots at them. The birds seemed untroubled by repeated discharges of the guns. Sometimes they would not leave until many of them were shot. During the years of abundance, the long-billed curlew appeared along the Atlantic Coast around mid-July, and offered gunners fine summer shooting.

Along the coasts, both long-billed and Eskimo curlews were often hunted from boats. Gunners rowed through the inlets and small bays, and intercepted the birds as they flew back and forth between feeding areas. Sometimes feeding flocks were stalked on sandbars and along tidal creeks. The boat was kept close to the shore to take advantage of whatever cover was available. Occasionally it was necessary to beach the boat and detour in order to come upon the birds from the rear.

On the Midwestern plains great numbers of Eskimo curlews were found, sometimes in the company of plover. Field glasses were often used by hunters to locate flocks of curlews. Densely packed groups of birds were visible at considerable distances, either on the ground or as the flocks circled before landing. A gunner might drive two or three miles by horse and buggy after locating a large flock through his field glasses. Then he would get as close as possible. When the sitting birds rose to their feet he would fire and perhaps fire again as the birds took flight.

As the spring wore on plover and curlews dispersed into

smaller flocks, and the fast-flying plover provided sporty shooting. Captain Bogardus, one of the great wingshots of the era, observed that a man who shot well on single plover was a good shot indeed. He preferred plover shooting after the flocks had broken up to any other wingshooting for practice purposes. Sometimes he engaged in this type of shooting before a tournament.

The greater and lesser yellowlegs remained on the game lists longer than some of the other species. They were still being hunted in the 1920s and 1930s. Alert and noisy, these birds earned the names telltale and tattler.

Yellowlegs were hunted on the beaches, tidal meadows and marshes. On a sandy beach a hole was often dug and seaweed piled around it to hide the gunner. In a marsh a blind was constructed out of brush; a substantial seat was placed in it for one or two men. Decoys of wood or tin would be set out if they were on the beach, facing into the wind and within easy range of the blind. The morning and afternoon seemed to be the preferred times for yellowlegs hunting. Decoys would be set out at daybreak for flights that began early and continued until midmorning. During midday, the gunner would sometimes fish offshore for species such as tomcod. The hunters would return around midafternoon for more shooting.

Most of the shorebirds were considered delicacies. Bogardus praised the upland plover as the most delicious meal of wild game in America. The Eskimo curlew was often referred to as "dough-bird." Its heavy layer of breast fat made it soft and pliable, like dough.

The rails, often referred to as "marsh hens," were really wading birds hunted from boats along coastal rivers and marshes. Several species—king, clapper, sora—were abundant and were widely sought for market and for sport. Their breeding range is extensive. One species or another is found in nearly every state. Rail shooting was perhaps most popular, however, along the Atlantic Coast. The Eastern tidal marshes were the setting for the quiet, moody paintings of Thomas Eakins, whose pictures of shorebird shooting were authentic representations of American hunting life of those times.

Rail shooting did not require great skill, for the slow, leg-dangling flight of the birds made them easy targets for a man armed with an open-bored gun charged with fine shot. It did require good balance, for the gunner would stand in the bow of a small, flat-bottomed boat as it was pushed through the tall reeds at high tide. Sometimes he might sit on a stool, but the unstable boat made shooting difficult if the hunter had to turn to take a bird rising on his opposite side. When the pusher called a right or a left, the gunner had to turn quickly but smoothly to avoid upsetting the craft or depositing himself in the water. Then he had to hit the bird as it skimmed the tops of the reeds.

Early hunters armed with muzzleloaders might use two guns if the shooting was fast. When barrels became hot from firing, a single spark could cause an accident while loading, and fouling made the process of recharging more difficult. Paper cartridges holding premeasured charges of powder and shot were carried in a box in the front of the boat for convenience and speed. A basket to hold the birds was usually taken along in the boat, as well as a supply of ice to cool the throats of the gunner and his pusher.

Successful rail shooting required a good pusher. Good, experienced men who poled rail boats were highly prized. The task demanded both strength and dexterity, for the boat had to move at a smooth, steady pace to allow the hunter to shoot as the birds flushed. A good pusher was also skilled at marking fallen birds, for several were often down at one time in the reeds. A good pusher who located downed rail could contribute much to the size of a day's bag, and experienced pushers commanded good wages for difficult work—as much as $2.50 or $3 an outing during the middle years of the nineteenth century.

Most of the birds that declined during the years of unlimited shooting were given total protection. The snipe, that elusive target of the bogs, was restored to the game lists. Today, it still offers great shooting opportunities.

Veteran snipe hunters often hunted without dogs by walking downwind so that rising birds were likely to give them crossing shots. The birds flushed against the wind, and a man positioned on the windward side was apt to get a good opportunity. Bogardus liked to hunt them in the spring, after the birds had grown fat from feeding in the rich bottomlands. In later years, many hunters decoyed snipe on open mud flats.

An effective technique involved two men hunting together. Two gunners walking downwind 30 or 40 yards apart were virtually certain to kill most of the birds that rose between them (provided they were good shots). Birds that scattered ahead of them were apt to present crossing shots to one gunner, depending on the direction of the wind. Bogardus warned against shooting snipe too quickly. He advised hunters to wait until the flight of the bird had straightened out. He suggested a ten-bore gun for snipe shooting, loaded with five drams of powder and one and a quarter ounces of No. 12 shot.

With the exception of the relatively few sportsmen who hunt snipe and rails, shorebird hunting is now a sport of the past. Perhaps this was inevitable, for excessive market hunting, and the widespread destruction of habitat contributed to the decline of the shorebirds. The years of great shorebird hunting in America were colorful and fascinating. They should be remembered for what they can tell us about our land, our history and ourselves. §

# The Drift and Float for Trout

*Richard L. Henry*

THE LONG, graceful cast epitomizes the art of fly fishing, but to know how to cast a fly is not necessarily to know how to deliver it well. In many instances delivery largely determines how the fly will perform. From a fish's viewpoint, of course, the appeal of your offering materializes only after the feathers reach the water. But then, whether the fly is animated or drifted with the current, its behavior reflects the real art of fishing with a fly.

The dry-fly angler working a small Catskill stream has little in common with the distance specialist heaving a streamer across a Western river. Their approach and delivery usually differ as much as their choice of tackle, yet the success of each lies in his ability to make his flies appeal to fish.

As a youth I carried flies but rarely used them unless I'd failed with bait and felt that nothing else would work. One day I was on a stream near my home and, aside from one small brook trout that swallowed my bait around daybreak, I hadn't had a touch all morning. By noon the May sun became warm and I chose the shade of a small bridge to rest and eat my lunch. Before unwrapping my sandwich, however, I tied on a nondescript nymph I'd bought and tossed it under the bridge. Minutes later, as the fly hung in the swift current just under the surface, a 15-inch brown grabbed it and nearly pulled the rod from my hand.

The catch seemed purely accidental because the dragging fly was unrealistic. Yet several years later when I fished only with flies, I found the downstream hang a valuable tactic, particularly on slow days. It can be fished at any depth as a single fly or a two- or three-fly cast in any combination of wet flies, streamers, or nymphs. Unlike most other techniques, it requires more patience than skill, and when a strike comes, the fish usually hooks itself.

I find the downstream hang even more effective, however, when retrieved slowly. Once the cast has straightened out downstream, I let the flies drag without imparted motion for a minute or two. Then I slowly retrieve a foot of line and pause again, continuing this pace until the flies are recast. Sometimes even big fish find it hard to resist the dragging wet flies.

One day several years ago Ellwood Gettle, Clarence Reichard, and I were finding few fish rising on a small Pennsylvania stream. Discouraged and uncomfortable in the summer heat, we found relief in the shade of a huge oak tree whose branches overhung the water. While I rested on the bank, my two friends switched from dries to wets so that they could relax on a mid-stream boulder and continue to fish the pool below. I remember that Ellwood chastised Clarence for hanging a Brown Hackle downstream because, according to Ellwood, the fly was never effective used that way. I remember too that 10 minutes later a huge trout swam away with Clarence's fly and some leader.

Few angling techniques, of course, are as simple as the

downstream hang. The delivery of a talented dry-fly angler, for example, may seem similar to that of a novice merely trying to get his fly on the water. But there's a distinction to be made between purpose and chance. Floating a dry fly without drag is a most difficult skill, and it is achieved by *controlled* slack in line and leader. But in bungling hands, a fly delivered with loose coils of line and leader will find few takers.

Limestone spring creeks are the dry-fly angler's greatest challenge. Clear, cold, and fertile, they glide silently through thick beds of aquatic vegetation and their trout grow heavy on an abundance of insects. But the slick currents are deceiving. Unlike most quiet water in freestone streams, the smooth surface creates a tug-of-war for any but the most carefully delivered dry fly. And along with this, the fish are as discriminating of fly pattern as any to be found.

I'm no stranger to spring creeks. I've spent thirty years testing the frustrating currents of some of Pennsylvania's best known limestoners. The Letort, near Carlisle, is probably the toughest; Falling Springs, about 30 miles to the west, runs a close second. And lying somewhere between the two, Big Spring was probably the trickiest of all as I knew it in the early 1950's. Beset by pollution problems, however, the Spring is now a second-rate trout stream.

To catch a trout rising in a typical spring creek requires first that you know the fish's observation lie as well as its taking position so that the fly won't be delivered behind the fish. Next, you must take the most advantageous casting position. An oozing mud bottom can make wading difficult or even impossible, so that compromise is often necessary. If you are by now within casting range of the fish and it is still feeding, there is yet another problem—drifting the fly over the trout without drag. And that means being able to cast sufficient slack to off-set the pull of the current.

There are two popular ways of executing a slack cast. One

is to underpower the delivery high over the water causing both line and leader to fall back in loose coils; the other is to check the forward cast sharply so that line and leader recoil in a manageable drift. Each technique has its place, depending on an angler's tastes and choice of tackle, and each serves to give the fly time to reach the target before drag begins.

Vince Marinaro is widely regarded as the most knowledgeable chalk-stream angler in the country, having designed innovative fly patterns that still remain popular today. But Marinaro's skills aren't confined to a fly-tyer's vise. On central Pennsylvania's spring creeks and particularly on the Letort, where most of his patterns were developed, his ability to achieve long, drag-free drifts is without peer.

I've had the privilege of fishing with Vince Marinaro numerous times and can attest to his being able to solve near-impossible angling problems. But one particular performance stands out. We were on the Tulpehocken Creek in southeastern Pennsylvania finding few fish moving that summer afternoon. While wandering about, however, I spotted a brown rising in an eddy across the stream. Reaching the trout would have required casting over a current that surged between heavy beds of elodea; and to complicate matters, the fish lay on the far side of the eddy where the current was going upstream. A background of trees ruined any chance of casting from the other bank. Believing that my best effort would be futile, I called to Vince for an opinion.

"Wouldn't be bad from the other side," Vince agreed after studying his options, "but it's worth a try from here." Having moved slightly upstream to help offset the pull of the current that lay between him and the fish, he began to false cast, using far more line than was necessary to reach his target. The delivery was allowed to die high over the stream; wide loops of line fell to the water and the fly landed lightly among tight coils of leader. The current immediately pulled at the line, but all the while the fly was unraveling from the slack in the leader and drifting toward the fish. With scarcely a second remaining before drag was inevitable, the trout rose to the fly and was hooked.

The phenomenal drift was made possible with what Vince calls a "puddle cast," an exaggerated use of the underpowered delivery. Although few can even hope to approach Marinaro's casting skills, most are capable of performing the cast well

enough to make a creditable showing on difficult currents. Along with being able to control slack in the cast, it's best to work at close range whenever possible, and a stiff-action rod allows better control than one of slow action, particularly when trying to reach difficult spots that require considerable force in delivery.

The slack cast is also useful when dead-drifting a wet fly or nymph. On moving water some slack is usually necessary if

you want the fly to sink; just how much depends primarily on your position and the uniformity and speed of the current. The dead drift, of course, is meant to suggest those insects that are carried with the current; and the greater your fly's freedom, the more natural it will appear to fish. So if weight is required to sink the fly, it's better pinched to a leader knot than tied into the body where it will hamper drift.

Tumbled along in the current with weight, a fly is consistently effective because it is taken to a depth where trout spend most of their time—on or near the bottom. The cast is made quartering or directly upstream with slack, the line mended if necessary to help overcome drag. As the fly drifts toward you, absolute control of recovered line is essential.

Holding the line loosely against the rod grip with the middle finger of the rod hand eliminates line sag between the stripping guide and the other hand, and keeping the rod tip close to the water makes it easier to strike a fish quickly. Handled this way, a nymph is a good way to test unfamiliar water.

I recall an autumn day on the Hoback River in northwestern Wyoming. New to the river, I waded into a boulder-studded pool with cautious optimism, then worked my way upstream with a dry No. 12 Adams. Rising fish were few, however, and by the time I'd covered a quarter-mile stretch I'd taken only several small cutthroats. Turning around, I went over the same water with a downstream cast of wet flies and streamers. Except for an ambitious 1-pounder that tried to swallow my Yellow Marabou, there was little evidence to dispute what I'd been told: most of the trout had already been taken.

Discouraged, I quit for lunch, then decided to make another effort. I tied a No. 12 Muskrat Nymph to a .007 tippet, pinching a tiny piece of lead to the leader knot closest to my fly. Then I waded into the same stretch where I'd begun to fish that morning, and cast my nymph upstream behind a submerged boulder. As the fly drifted toward me the line hesitated, and when I tightened up I was into a fish. I didn't land that one, but by the time I'd worked my beat on the river I'd taken seven cutthroats on my nymph. Between 1 and 2 pounds, the trout were hardly trophies, but they saved the river's reputation.

Being able to detect the take of a free-drifting fly under-water is nearly as important as the drift. Some anglers use a buoyant dry fly as a dropper 3 feet up the leader. Functioning as a bobber, the fly signals any unnatural movement in the drift. Others prefer a bright wet pattern on the dropper as an indicator. But most skilled anglers use neither, relying on their ability to follow the course of either the line or the leader, the length of the cast largely determining which one.

In the slack behind large boulders or wherever there is slow water between two merging currents, a downstream cast is often the best approach. Having cast below where the currents meet, pull the fly back until it settles to the bottom of the pocket. Once there, it can be crawled over the gravel unaffected by the general flow of the stream. The obvious advantage of this position is that the rate of retrieve is controlled entirely by the angler. Although there are no absolute rules, a pull of sev-eral inches every 5 seconds isn't too slow.

IT'S EASY TO BECOME ADDICTED to tumbling a fly along the bot-tom because it so often works. But in the transformation stage from nymph to adult, many mayfly-types drift to the surface to shed their shucks. Once they're plentiful enough to draw the attention of fish, the duns are the forms to be matched. But in the early part of a hatch, the nymphs are most often taken ris-ing to the surface well off the streambed.

I learned long ago that nymphs aren't always best drifted along the bottom. One evening I found pale sulphur duns com-ing off and the trout, I thought, were rising to them. I had no reason to question the tastes of the fish until I'd failed with sev-eral proven dry patterns. Baffled, I waded to midstream, crouching low and trying to spot what I believed to be a less conspicuous insect and the answer to my problem. Instead I saw only sulphur nymphs coming to the surface. Then it occurred to me that the fish might be taking insects just underneath. Having changed to an imitation of the sulphur nymph, I began to hook trout that had refused my dry flies.

Streamers are designed to look like small fish, and their fish appeal lies in your ability to make them suggest the movements of forage fish common to a particular stream. Casting a streamer across stream and teasing it slowly against the currents no doubt accounts for most of the fish taken on this type fly. But you'll find there are times when dead-drifting a streamer will take trout too.

I remember a day in late April when Pennsylvania's Tobyhanna Creek was high and cold, fed by patches of melting snow that still lingered along its banks. Working our way downstream through a long piece of broken water, Ellwood Gettle and I had raised several fish but hooked none on streamers. But when we reached the Home Pool, a long, slow-moving stretch, Ellwood hooked two trout. As he netted the second, I asked about fly pattern.

"Yellow Marabou, the same as you're using," he said. "But they want it on a dead drift. Turn around and see what happens." Taking his advice, I began to cast upstream and was soon into a 12-inch brown. In fact, for the rest of the afternoon trout grabbed our free-drifting streamers often enough to turn an otherwise dull day into one of reasonable success.

Big water is often tough to fish. Deep pools and strong currents restrict wading, making it difficult to get a fly deep enough to score. I've never cared for sinking lines, but a forward taper designed to sink the first 10 feet along with mending will help get you down. And any time my casts average 50 feet or more I use a stripping basket, coiling the line directly into the basket. On shorter casts I retrieve and store the line in my left hand, using the hand-twist method.

I prefer long leaders for fishing on top and relatively short ones when working underneath. A 14-footer tapered to .006 is about right for casting a No. 14 dry fly; refined to .004 and a No. 24, the leader would be about 18 feet. On the other hand, a leader from 6 to 7½ feet will sink the fly better than a longer one. Whatever its length, however, it should be heavy enough in the butt section to turn over easily when you want it to.

The way you drift or retrieve your fly is far more important than either its size or pattern. So before you become submerged in the academic judgment of fly selection, learn the fundamentals of making the fly's actions appeal to fish. How you handle your feathers is the true measure of your angling skills. §

# Roll-Your-Own Fishing

*Vance Bourjaily*

T HE MOST exciting fish I ever brought out of the water took me two years to catch.

I finally got it on a lusterless, old, machine-tied, Japanese white streamer fly, using a workaday, eight-foot flyrod, the maker's name long since worn away. It was equipped with one of those small-boy, skeleton flyreels, without click or drag, a frayed silk line that didn't float anymore, and, for leader, about 20 inches of undifferentiated monofilament snipped off the end of the supply on an abandoned spincast reel.

My cast, if that's the word, was a 15-footer. I let the old fly sink away, started to retrieve slowly, overhand, and the fish appeared, drifting upward toward the lure, opening its mouth just under the surface, sucking in and hooking itself.

There were a couple of bullfrogs watching. They didn't move. It was 3 o'clock of a hot afternoon.

My fish, as I eased it in, was seven, well, six, inches long. It fought with all the ferocity of a lady finger being slid from the whipped cream and strawberries of a charlotte russe. It looked up at me from the shallow water at my feet, goggling at, I think, the sheer incomprehensibility of what was happening.

I looked back, grinning in absolute joy. I knelt, wet my left hand, took the little thing off the hook and sent it swimming away with a whispered word of benediction. Then I whooped like a drunk cowboy, dropped the rod, jumped up in the air, turned, and ran all the way down to our farmhouse, half a mile away, to tell the family:

"They survived. We've got a walleye population."

This was in the fourth of the five ponds we've built and stocked with fish on our Iowa farm, and if the fishing memories, some a little more conventionally dramatic, mostly belong to spring and summer evenings, the story of each pond would start with winter dreaming.

THE FIRST WAS CONCEIVED on a February afternoon, and not by me. I would have to admit, as a matter of fact, that I found it inconceivable to begin with.

It came into the conversation as my wife and I were being shown the land by a real estate man. The seller was along, too, and he was anxious. In his view the place was hilly and farmed out. It had a muddy creek flowing through the best field, a branch of the same creek flowing through another. It had a lot of timber land he hadn't been able to afford to clear, some places that were too steep to fence off, and several patches inaccessible except on foot. I'm not sure if he realized that some of these drawbacks were assets in our eyes: he kept pointing out commercial virtues he thought we might miss.

"Had corn right here, three, good, 100-bushel years," he was saying, as we climbed toward the highest land on the farm. "You could put it in beans now, and get a heck of a crop."

I wasn't much of a farmer, but even I knew, looking at the

eroded soil, that these hillsides needed to be put in pasture and would be, even so, a long time healing. And that a crop of soybeans would only loosen the dirt more and turn the ruts and washes into gullies. I replied with an unfriendly grunt, and the man changed the subject.

"Me and my brother was going to build a big pond here," he said. "Raise catfish. Now pond-raised catfish, that's the new thing. Sell'm to restaurants and supermarkets, they'll take all they can get."

"Weren't you telling me the creeks flood all over the bottom fields in the spring?" I asked.

"Well, not every spring. And like I say, when the water goes down, that silt's left with a world of fertilizer in it. Washes off the other fellow's field, right onto yours."

"How could you dam one of those creeks to make a pond? It would cost a million dollars."

"Couldn't do her for a million," he agreed.

"Then where were you and your brother going to hold the water for your catfish?" I asked. "Or were those cornfield catfish?"

"Right here, like I told you." He was pointing across about as dry-looking a gulch as I'd ever seen. Furthermore, it was a gulch full of trees, some of them quite large. The gulch was about 90 feet across and 20 deep, and it cut back between the hill we were standing on and the next hill over, its floor sloping up between them for a 100 yards or so until it split into two smaller gulches and disappeared into deep woods.

BEFORE I COULD ASK my man what sort of fool he took me for, he told me. "Why you just can't understand at all, can you?" he said, slowing his speech and separating each word distinctly. "Now: this here we are looking into, it is a main waterway. This here drains about 40 acres up above. What you have to do is clear the sides and bottom. Then you block it off with a clay dam from one sidehill to the other. See? You drop in a tube for the overflow, and you got her."

"Sure," I said. "And what do you do for water? Haul it up in buckets?"

"Didn't I just get done telling you?"

"Are you trying to say there's springs, or what?"

"Runoff. Runoff." He shook his head at my dimness. "Melt of snow and fall of rain. Drainin' down through the grassy roots, and all the little weedy waterways, and down between the trees in the timbers. . . ."

I swear I could smell it, when he said that. All that lovely soft rainwater, sifting through leaf-mold and around wild-flower stems dripping off limbs and seed-heads, gathering, and I almost missed the wonderful thing he said next:

"Believe you could get cost-sharing."

That was when I learned that the state and especially the Federal Government are more than casually interested in having farm ponds built, and that the Department of Agriculture may, if certain requirements are met, help pay for the building. Equally important, the Department will send along government engineers, my favorite public servants, to look at locations and do survey and design.

Nor is it inconsistent with my present purpose to add that, while getting its citizens to go fishing is not the Government's goal—its interest is in the soil conservation that results from water control—nevertheless, it will good-naturedly send along some fish when things are ready.

By our first summer on the farm, we had filed our application for help. The engineers had come out and agreed, to my slight chagrin, that the seller's spot was a fine one for a two-acre pond. We were approved; we solicited bids; we picked a contractor.

Daniel Keith Yoder was and is the contractor's name; he has built four of our five ponds, and I celebrate him here as a

Michelangelo of the bulldozer. Daniel Keith has an eye for dirt, for where to dig it, how to shape it, finish it, and dress the job. His work delights not only his customers but even the engineers whose designs he accomplishes. Other contractors they grumble at; Daniel Keith is their pet.

Most of what had to be cleared from the pond site was brush, box-elder, willow, cottonwood and aspen—nice things, but fast growing and plentiful on the farm. There were, on the other hand, half a dozen decent white oaks and a fine black cherry, but those I could take out with a chain saw, and would be glad to have for lumber. There were some straight young hickories, hardly more than poles, which I didn't want to lose, and there was the hackberry. It was the biggest one of its kind on the farm, a beautifully shaped shade tree of no great value as lumber, a relative of the dying elms but immune from the beetles that were killing them, a corky barked, silvery, big tree.

"Anything you don't want to salvage, we'll grub out and push into a pile. You can burn it or not," Daniel Keith said.

"Or leave it for a rabbit house," said my friend Tom, who was thinking of getting a beagle.

Daniel Keith walked off to set engineer flags around the projected water line.

"It's that hackberry, Tom," I said. "It must be 100 years old."

"You never get anything without giving up something else," Tom said.

Once the clearing was finished, they rolled back and made a pile of topsoil to use for dressing later. Then, just past the line the dam was to follow and down at what would be the base, Daniel Keith began, to my astonishment, to dig. What he dug was a trench, eight feet deep and ten feet wide, straight across the bottom of the gulch. This was to be packed with the best clay they could find, he explained, so that water couldn't work through the ground under the dam.

On the day he was to start packing the trench, my wife and I were walking up to watch when we heard the motors stop. All of them.

"That's ominous," Tina said, and we hurried. At the site, we saw that Daniel Keith was off his machine and down inside the trench. He looked up and saw us.

"Sand," he said, in the same tone of voice one might use in saying *scorpion* or *rattlesnake*. Sometime in the recent geological past, there'd been a watercourse down there, with a sandy bottom, just the sort of thing the trench was supposed to intercept but deeper, more extensive. "We'll need to get a dragline now," Daniel Keith said. "And see if we can get through the sand, dig it out. It'll cost you. If we can't get it all, we'll have to give up on this pond. The other thing we can do is fill it in and go away, not take the chance. It's up to you."

I'm not sure I said anything.

"Depends on how much a fellow wants a pond, I guess," said Daniel Keith sympathetically.

I looked over at the pile where my hackberry tree lay on its side, roots and all, with brush and young hickories piled against it. There was no thought involved.

That first pond, in those uninflated days, cost $2500. The Government paid a little over half.

What we had, when the machines rumbled off, was a deep, raw two-and-a-half acre basin, steepest and deepest where the dam blocked off the lower end. It was 21 feet down, from the brave little flags that marked the someday-waterline, and the question now was *how soon?* In late September we had a half-day's rain. I hurried up to the pond as soon as it ended and saw that the sides of the basin were scarred from little rivulets of water now collected at the bottom in a lot of mud and perhaps a 50-gallon puddle. At 326,000 gallons of water per acre foot, times two-and-a-half acres, and an average depth of eight feet, we didn't have much more than 5 million gallons to go. I thought it might take two or three years; it didn't. By the end of April there was water trickling out the overflow tube. By the middle of May it was roaring.

By June, though the pond was a mile away from our creeks, the nearest source of aquatic life, we'd begun to have an environment. Frogs and muskrats had found the pond. So had an aquatic plant with arrowhead-shaped leaves, and some marsh grass. There were waterbugs and dragonflies. A flock of lesser scaup had rested over one night, on their way north. And the next morning I was on my way in the pickup truck, answering a call from the Soil Conservation Service to pick up fish.

These were to be largemouth bass fry. Later I'd get some catfish, but for now it was 800 little bass, and I had, in the back, a clean, new, 30-gallon garbage can, two-thirds full of pond water, and held fast with log chains. I went slowly, so as not to lose water, and worried all the way about whether the can was big enough.

In front of the SCS office when I arrived, and already surrounded by others on the same errand, was a federal-green truck with built-in tanks and the name of a fish hatchery on the door. A couple of men in olive drab jackets and whipcord pants stood by, one of them with a list. I got out and approached just in time to hear my own name read out.

"Eight-hundred bass, no bluegills," said the man with the list, and the other one dipped into a tank with a graduated beaker which looked a good deal like my wife's one-pint, Pyrex measuring cup. He poured the water out, looked at the graduations, and poured back about half of what seemed to be a seething black mass of tiny organisms.

"Is that all of them?" I dipped a bucket of water from my garbage can and handed it up. What he held was three jiggers of fish.

"Probably a few extra," he said, emptied his beaker into my bucket and his partner called the next name. I drove slowly back to the farm. I remember pouring three jiggers of fish into 5-million gallons of water with a sense of total disbelief that I would ever see any of those bass again. But a year later they were five inches long, and we could see them clearly, swimming by in schools of 15 and 20. By then we'd added channel catfish, too.

It was fairly slow that first summer, and the fish still small. We did so much catching and releasing that my son still won't keep a fish (he eats the ones I catch). On calm evenings, they would take surface lures—poppers and flies and things like flyrod Flatfish. That same son bought me a gorgeous deer-hair frog for my birthday sending off to Orvis for it, which probably did the best of anything we used.

It will not surprise bass fishermen to hear that, in the third spring, when the fish were a foot long and more and guarding the nests, they would fight anything that came along, never mind how bright, how big, how noisy.

The fishing was nice, now, on summer evenings, particularly from a canoe with one paddling while the other cast.

It was fun. It was soothing. We built a second pond, the same size, but this time without cost-sharing. We left the timber standing in the upper end of the second one, something the engineers wouldn't have sanctioned, in order to create snags as the trees died naturally. This pond became the one in which snapping turtles congregated and wood ducks nested. It produced, after a couple of years and having been stocked from the first pond, larger bass—I couldn't understand why the snags would have that effect, and didn't learn how little they had to do with it until a really big fish came out of that second pond.

Now I am, of course, like anyone with a strong preference for the flyrod, totally indifferent to how large a fish I catch by comparison with other fishermen. So when a 15-year-old named Fred, fishing deep in midsummer with a lavender plastic worm, caught a four-and-a-half-pounder—still our homeplace record, and a sizable largemouth for Iowa—I naturally felt no resentment beyond wanting to break the child's thumbs. It really was a heck of a fish, and I have to admit that a good many lavender plastic worms got bumped along the bottom in the deep parts in the week that followed, and that some other pretty fair-sized bass came up. But it wasn't until I went back to my flyrod that I understood why this pond held bigger fish. I was using the hair frog, and what I got first was a remarkably hard strike from what looked, as it swirled, like an eight- or ten-inch bass. I managed to hook it. I'd filed the barb off my hook, and so brought the fish in rather quickly, expecting it to do some tail-dancing. Instead, it plunged and fought all the way, and, when I got it to hand, it turned out not to be a bass at all. It wasn't a catfish, either, the only other species we'd stocked. Instead, it was the fattest, brightest, healthiest-looking young bluegill I've ever seen.

How it got into the pond—along with quite a few others like it, as we soon learned—is anybody's guess. The most persuasive rationale I've heard is that they came airmail. It's said that fish eggs sometimes stick to the legs of waterfowl and are transported that way from pond to pond. Whatever the explanation, it's confirmation of the current attitude of fishery technicians: put in a bluegill population for forage fish, they say, if you want large bass.

Spring never came for our bass and bluegills, nor for our generally forgotten catfish, either. We went off traveling that winter, not that our presence on the farm would have prevented what happened. It's called winter-kill. The ponds froze, as they always do, but the weather was more severe than usual, the ice thicker, the snow heavier and longer-lasting.

We returned in March, as the thaw was starting, and on the first day back I visited both ponds. There were dead catfish, two and three feet long, all around the margins of the ice, and hundreds of raccoon tracks. The coons were cleaning up the carcasses as fast as they could, contesting them with a good number of crows.

I was sad, of course, and yet we wouldn't miss the catfish. We'd stopped fishing for them, because the pond-raised kind were muddy tasting, and we'd seen them only when, occasionally, one would hit some sort of bass lure—they liked one called a Johnson Silver Minnow. In any case, whatever hope I'd had that the bass might have survived disappeared in the next few days. It took the bass bodies, for some reason, a little longer than the catfish to start floating to the surface.

I asked around, looking for consolation, and found people willing to declare that the winter-kill phenomenon was exceptional, unlikely to happen again. Impatient to restore our pleasure, one that friends and neighbors enjoyed as much as we did, I restocked with catchables—foot-long bass from a commercial hatchery, 100 of them, I think, at $1 each.

My friend Tom tried all his bamboo rods in turn that summer at the ponds. The kid, Fred, came back, 17 now, and couldn't catch anything bigger than anyone else could. My daughter was old enough to cast with ultralight spinning gear, and caught her first fish. Not to mention her second, third, fourth. . . . I got a deer-hair crayfish for my birthday this time. . . . Winter came, the second after the winter-kill, and I learned that we were in a cycle of hard winters. We lost our fish again.

We had built, meanwhile, a really large pond—an eight-acre affair—at the west end of our farm, after selling off some of the land up there. Because of its size, this pond is winter-proof, and we had stocked it, like the very first, with government-donated bass and catfish fry. After the second winter-kill, I went to the big west pond, just before spawning time, and caught mature, gravid bass to restock with. They took. They reproduced. After another summer's wait, we had fishing again in the original ponds. I learned about a device that might prevent winter-kill—windmill driven propellors, floated in rubber rings. They keep an area of water open, thus admitting light and oxygen. They cost, well, not as much as a fishing vacation in Argentina, but, for me anyway, close: they cost $350 each, and I now had three ponds to worry about. The first, the second, and a new one, the most beautiful of all. Feeling flush, we'd built the woods pond just a year before, along with still another—a half-acre, very deep pond with steep sides, near the buildings. A swimming pond. This swimming pond, in which few plants grow, had no fish, either, and so was not a worry. But in the new woods pond, and contrary to all reasonable advice, I'd stocked walleyes—not a pond fish they said.

It was a deep, well-shaded pond, about an acre around, and the prettiest of all. Wood ducks loved it, and so did we. Stubbornly, I bought 250 little walleyes; I knew they wouldn't reproduce, but I thought that, with luck, they might survive. I got them in August 1978. The year that must be specified because the winter of 1978-79 was the worst in the midwest since 1935.

As that winter got worse and worse, as the ice thickened and the snow deepened, I thought a lot about fish. I thought about them as creatures for which I'd created certain worlds, in which I had put them to grow. I did not think of them as having minds or feelings, but as a form of life I'd fostered which now, individual by individual, would die—not in pain, I thought, or despair—but as victims, nevertheless of a kind of wantonness, and the wanton was me, I assumed, as Tina and I brought our flocks and herds through the bitter weather, my third fish-kill, and did not suppose I would want to restock a fourth time—not until the windmills could be bought, anyway, and perhaps I was too discouraged by now even to believe in windmills.

There came the spring of '79, and yes, coon tracks around the ponds. And yes, I found a small, dead walleye by the woods pond one morning, and after that stopped looking. I didn't want to see dead fish again. Let the coons and the crows have them. 'Bye, fish.

But we still loved our ponds. If fish couldn't survive in the cycle of hard winters, the ponds were still beautiful and the waterfowl and deer and all the other wildlife used them. Windmills might be afforded sometime, or some new technology come along. The snapping turtles had delicious meat in them, and we all loved frog legs.

It was August 1979. About frogs: I don't think of gathering them as a sport, only a harvesting operation. Gigging them at night has no appeal for me. What I've settled on for frogging is a 22 with long-rifle cartridges. These knock a frog out instantly and completely, if they hit at all. So I was slipping along the bank of the second pond, rifle in hand, looking carefully for the next bullfrog, when, glancing into shallow water, I saw fish. I took another step, and checked myself. Fish? I crouched, and looked back, and there they were. Bass. Survivors. Reproducers. That was my first yell of the day. I may even have done a little dance. The next yell, I've described. It came after I'd run back, put the frogs in the refrigerator, swapped the rifle for my nondescript bugging rod, and run to the woods pond. That was the day I caught the little walleye, and learned that most of them, too, seemed to have survived. And now I am waiting for another summer, fairly certain that the walleyes have come through the winter just now passing as I write.

And so my fishing fantasy is much in mind as the ground thaws. It has no trout in it, or muskies or landlocked salmon, no tuna, marlin, swordfish. It takes place in just a few weeks, now, in a small pond to which I may have access—Knowling's or Zach's or perhaps a certain quarry. The fish, of course, are bluegills, 15 or 20 pair, mature, ready to spawn. I'll get them, keep them alive, put them in.

Then in August, it will be another white streamer fly, a

hushed moment and, as the fantasy goes, another walleye, a year older than the last. Even so it will not be eating size. It will be, I think, what walleye fishermen call a "hammer handle."

I wrote about a fifth pond, small and deep, near the buildings, which we use for swimming. It's unusually clear for a farm pond, because of the steep sides, and the water, 28 feet down, must be really cold.

No one is going to encourage me to carry out this plan, and it will take another $500 which I may or may not ever feel I can cut loose, but before I'm done with pond-making, I've got to try trout again. Once, long ago, I answered an ad for "farm pond adapted trout fingerlings," bought a couple of hundred, put them in a pond, never saw one again. But I don't think the problem was temperature so much as oxygen.

So: What I think of now, more often than I ought, is a device called a GenAIRator, made by some people in Wisconsin, which is designed to aerate lakes and ponds. It consists of an electric air pump which you're supposed to fasten to a tree or post on the shore. It feeds air through plastic pipe to a venturi tube, down at the bottom of the pond. The function of the venturi is to send a stream of air bubbling up to the surface, and I assume that this will both give oxygen and, as that cold bottom layer of water is raised up, lower the temperature at the surface.

I don't know for certain that this will enable me to raise trout. I don't know if the windmills would work. I don't know, for that matter, that my walleyes will go on living through hot Augusts as they grow large, or that my bass won't die again. But fish are like other crops, it seems to me now. You fix up an environment, you plant, cultivate, protect as best you can, and with luck—and a white streamer, or a deer-hair frog, or even a lavender plastic worm—you harvest. For food, sometimes. For fun, more often. For the feeling of putting into the world a good thing that wasn't there before. §

# Back in Birds

*Geoffrey Norman*

W HEN YOU HUNT BIRDS, you do not have to get up at dawn in order to have breakfast. Frank poured a second cup of coffee for himself and one for me. We had already eaten fried eggs, biscuits, and hot country sausage.

"Supposed to be a lot of birds this year," he said. "I talked to a fellow up in the north end of the county, where I used to hunt, and he says he hasn't ever seen so many birds."

"Maybe we ought to drive up to the north end of the county then," I said.

"Nah. Too far. Anyway, there will be plenty of birds around here. I've got a couple of places picked out."

"You've got all the birds named and numbered, too. Right?"

"Not this year. I haven't scouted that much. Been too busy. Seems like I'm too busy to breathe these days. But I can't see where I'm getting all that much done—and I damned sure ain't making any money."

"Running hard just to stay in place?"

"I wish. Anyway, here it is bird season, and I haven't scouted any birds. I haven't shot a gun since last season. But I have worked the dogs. They're ready even if I'm not."

"It's been years for me," I said. "I hope I don't embarrass the dogs."

"Don't think it hasn't happened. I remember a day when I just could not shoot for some damned reason. Couldn't have hit a bull in the ass with a bass fiddle."

Didn't sound likely. I'd never seen anyone who could shoot like Frank could. When he was fourteen he could out-shoot all the grown men in a dove field. He was born to handle a shotgun the way Joe Namath was born to throw a football.

"I was having a bad day, you know. Happens to every-body." He smiled. "You must have a bad day every now and then in the city. Well, after I'd missed about seven straight birds that day, the dogs just sort of walked away and started trotting around the woods like a couple of poodles in the park. Didn't want to have anything to do with me."

"Well, then, I hope I can still shoot."

"Comes right back to you. Don't worry. You want another cup, or do we get up out of these chairs and hunt?"

We got up and walked outside, where the tall yellow pines were shedding the way they do every fall. There were two dogs behind a stretched wire fence in the corner of the yard. Both were setters, one black-and-white and the other almost all white with a few red freckles. They were old but eager, pawing and barking and trying to climb the fence. "Those two are ready," Frank said. "They're going to run hard. You haven't forgotten how to walk in the city, have you?"

WE DROVE DOWN THE COUNTRY ROADS, past small patch farms and several stands of regimentally planted pines. It was about nine o'clock. The deer hunters had been out since before dawn, and most of them would be coming back out of the woods in an hour or two, when the football fans would be mixing the first Bloody Marys and checking the television reception.

We pulled off the road and followed a gravel drive around a small pecan orchard into the back yard of the kind of brick bungalow that has replaced old frame farmhouses everywhere. We knocked and a man came to the door. He was thick and smooth, with small eyes and big hands that were twisted and bony. Frank introduced me, and I shook hands with the man. He gripped my hand the same way that he would grip the handle on a shovel.

"You boys fixing to hunt some birds?"

Frank nodded. "We wanted to ask if we could hunt some of your land. I know it's posted."

"Not to you. That's just to keep out the sons of bitches who bust up fences. You go on and hunt. You ought to find some birds. I just got through combining, and there's beans scattered in those fields."

We thanked the man and drove to a field covered with broomweed. There were some blackjack oaks and a few wind-seeded pines standing in the field like sentries. A wash that ran off to one side was filled with blackberry brambles.

The sun had come clear of the tree line, and a steady breeze stirred the pines. Three or four fields away, a lone hawk cruised the breeze as though it were an interstate, going five minutes between wingbeats. He dove once and came up empty.

The dogs went to work, and we walked behind them. The first stiffness passed; my legs felt limber and strong. The little six-pound shotgun, a side-by-side twenty, seemed just right. I felt great. I was one bird hunter who could walk all day long.

"That black-and-white dog is onto something," Frank said. The dog had stopped cold and was holding steady as stone except for his tail, which stood straight out and quivered

like a man fighting an impulse to murder. The other dog came up behind him, saw the point, and froze to honor it. "Tell me that ain't beautiful," Frank said softly.

We walked up to them through the waist-high grass, guns ready. We passed the first dog, and he held point. As we stepped even with the black-and-white, the covey came up. There was a single ragged explosion and then a blur of fragments angling off in a dozen directions. Old reflexes moved the gun to my shoulder, and the barrel covered a single bird moving almost straightaway—the easiest shot. I touched the trigger, and the bird dropped cleanly. The second bird was almost out of range and moving to the right, boring hard for the brambles. I missed.

Frank had hit with both barrels. The dogs brought the

birds to him, and he tossed me mine with a soft underhand motion. The bird was a cock with brown body feathers and white on his crown and around his chest. A stately little bird, this bobwhite, and as I noticed the faint beads of blood that oozed through his feathers, I felt the touch of sadness that is the paradox of all hunting. I put the bird in the game pouch of my vest and wiped my hand on my leg.

We hunted the singles, most of them in the brambles, and we each shot a bird. We left the rest and went looking for another covey. There were two more in that field, and all the birds we shot had a crop full of soybeans.

Soybean agriculture has been great for game. There are more birds now than when the farmers planted cotton. Still, you don't shoot every bird in a covey. The foxes will get some, and the hawks will get some. House cats that have been turned out into the woods will get some. Disease and cold will kill some. A few will be hit by cars, and about the same number will be shot. A few birds from every covey will survive all of that—if they aren't overhunted—and in the spring, the cocks will fight for turf and strut for hens. They will pair and breed and nest. And there will be birds again in the fall.

"I told you we'd have birds," Frank said. "You could get them here all through the season, too. But I don't like to work a covey too hard. You've got to know when to quit."

We stopped at midday, tired, hungry, and dry. We drove to a general store where we ate sardines and soda crackers, drank cold tea on the porch, and talked with the owner. The day had turned hot, and I thought of all those people dressed up and drunk for a football game.

"I am sure glad you came," Frank said. "Otherwise I might have missed all this."

"You? Somebody would have to break your legs to keep you out of the woods on opening day—or any other day."

He smiled. "Not anymore."

"You must have cut forty days of school to go hunting. They were always calling your parents."

"I was kind of a buck. It's true."

"And you were the first boy in our group to get a summons."

"Shooting wood ducks after dark. It's the only time you can shoot them. But I'm not proud of that. I don't even hunt ducks anymore. If you hunt public land, there are so many hunters you have to draw blinds in a lottery. If you want to hunt private clubs, you need about two producing oil wells. I just like to get up and go."

We paid for lunch, and the dogs jumped back into the bed of the truck. We were all a little tired now that we'd had time to cool down and stiffen up. The first fifteen minutes of the new field were hard. The twenty-gauge felt heavy now, and my legs were no longer supple and responsive. Frank moved crisply and his example carried all of us. Before long I was revived, and the dogs were back in birds.

We shot all afternoon. First the covey rise and then the singles. Never too many. When we walked, we watched the dogs and talked about this and that.

"You know why I still like to hunt quail?" Frank said. It was near the end of the day, and the dogs were tired. "Because there's more to it than just rolling up the score. I used to count the ducks and the deer. I even won some pretty big money betting on myself in a dove field. But I don't even know how many birds we've shot today. I'm pretty sure we're under the limit, yet I couldn't give you an exact count on a bet. I don't know if it's because I'm older or smarter or lazier, but what I like to do these days is fool around with the dogs and shoot a few birds. I know two things I never knew when I was a kid. I know how to take it slow, and I know when to quit."

We were through hunting now, just walking through the woods on our way back to the car. The sounds of the night creatures were beginning to rise. Long, ragged flights of black-birds passed overhead. The air was cool and laced with the fragrance of pine, which you do not smell at any other time of day.

We drove back to the house, where we cleaned the birds, fed the dogs, bathed, and drank bourbon. Frank's wife put the birds in a Dutch oven and smothered them with onions. I ate four or five. The kids sat in another room of the house, watching something on the television. We did the dishes, and when the children were in bed, we drank another glass of bourbon and watched the late news. I recognized the usual Saturday night material—murders, traffic accidents, football riots. Frank turned the set off and yawned. "You know," he said, "I once came about an inch from going to reform school, but damned if I don't feel like the only civilized man in all of Alabama right now. Good night, friend. Tomorrow we'll hunt more birds." §

# Still-Water Trout

*David Seybold*

S EVERAL AUTUMNS AGO I stood on the shore of a favorite New England brook trout lake and watched a school
of spawning trout dimple the surface 100 feet in front of me. I
was a newcomer to the area, and to the mysteries of lake fishing. Before me lay the open lake, with all the telltale signs I
was used to hidden beneath the surface. Where were the ed-
dies? Where were the bends and ripples? The fast water, slow
water? The whole lake was one giant pool, and I was completely helpless in understanding any of it.

Still, I had fished ponds and lakes before, so schooling
brook trout were not uncommon to me. But the trout I was
watching were behaving in a manner I had never seen before.
These fish progressed down the shoreline for 100 yards without
varying their course or fanning out into the lake. They moved
along a distinct line that began to my right and ended to the
left. Without pausing, they dimpled the surface, apparently
feeding in the film, for 25 yards, went down for perhaps a min-

ute, quietly reappeared slightly farther down the shoreline, went along for another 25 yards, and then vanished.

Now the lake became still in the chilly autumn air. Its surface held its breath and reflected the last of the foliage in the surrounding hillsides. Without the trout dimpling the surface, all became flat and austere, as if no living thing had ever existed there. Like paintings in a museum after it has closed for the day, all things contiguous to the lake became hushed and colorless, the tarnished-gray sky casting a pallor over the countryside.

Entranced by the somber stillness of the scene before me, I totally forgot about the schooling trout and their curious behavior. But then something caught my eye and usurped the stillness. It was another school of trout, and it appeared in the same area as the previous school. This time I did not lose my senses to the season, however. I watched as the trout proceeded down the shoreline in the exact manner as their predecessors. But when they "vanished," I waited and kept scanning the line of water that they seemed to move along. And after several minutes had elapsed, sure enough, more trout appeared in the same spot to my right, and behaved in the same fashion.

Although I was pleased that more trout had appeared, I was perplexed as to *why* they had. To my novice eyes, there was no reason for them to behave as they were. But something was happening out there, even if I did not know what it was.

To compound the problem, I did not have a boat and the water was too deep for me to wade within flycasting range. Fortunately I have always rated watching trout just behind catching trout, so I was content to continue my observations.

As I watched the trout, I felt as if I were attending the performance of a one-act play—with the same act being repeated again and again. A school of trout would appear to my right, step up and sashay across the set like well-rehearsed bathing beauties, then exit stage-left. It was as if every trout in the lake was making its debut. So many trout paraded by me that day that I honestly thought I had seen the lake's entire population. But, of course, I had not.

That memorable afternoon occurred at the end of October ten years ago, and it marked for me the beginning of an ongoing study into the habits of brook trout in still water. What I saw on that day, I since have seen literally hundreds of times. And although I still do not have answers that completely satisfy me as to *why* brook trout behave as they do in the lake I fish, I now know how to use their behavior to my advantage.

Depending on the region, brook trout begin to come up from the depths of ponds and lakes to spawn from early September to early November. At first they gather in tight schools and cruise shorelines and, if any exist, mouths of inlets and outlets. It is during this initial schooling period that they are most susceptible to the angler's offerings.

Until the moment arrives when the water temperature and photoperiod (the number of daylight hours) are just right and the trout pair off to complete their odyssey, which can take several days to a week, they will feed voraciously, debauching themselves on almost anything that crosses their path. This feasting is shortlived, however, for with each day that the schools remain intact, the trout become less interested in stuffing themselves and more concerned with procreation.

The lake that I fish is a 606-acre jewel neatly tucked into the heart of the Dartmouth/Lake Sunapee region of New Hampshire. It is a deep lake with many springs, and it supports a large and healthy brook trout population. There is one outlet and one major inlet, with several others appearing during spring runoff and after heavy rains. The major inlet is often too low for trout to run up in the fall, and they are forced to spawn in the lake itself.

Anglers who fish the lake during the autumn season (it is flyfishing-only from the day after Labor Day to October 15) usually troll streamers or wet flies. They know the trout are in schools and cruising along the shoreline. But because there are no suitable tributaries for spawning, many anglers think the trout keep moving around the lake, and that the best way to catch them is to constantly troll. The only time they will still-fish is when the trout are visibly close to shore. Unfortunately, it can be very difficult to catch them by then. Either the trout are on the verge of spawning, and the last thing on their minds is food, or they have already spawned and are not yet feeding again.

About the only chance an angler has of catching fish in either of these two stages is to agitate them into striking, which they will do in anger or from habit. And although this method does work, it often requires an inordinate amount of casting.

There is, I am relieved to say, another way to catch these trout of autumn. It is far less exhausting, it can save on gasoline and terminal tackle, and if done correctly, it can stop the angler from pulling out his hair over fish he can see but cannot get to strike—at anything!

After ten years of stumbling, mumbling and finally figuring out a few of the clues that trout in my lake leave, I have come to realize that they do not cruise around the lake at all! Instead, they come up from the depths, find a section of shoreline that has the necessities for spawning—spring areas, underwater currents, sandbars, sandy shoals, gravelly reefs—and then cruise back and forth and out in front of it. What I was seeing that first afternoon was the same school moving back and forth, right to left. And what I could not see was the way they were returning to where I first saw them, which they did by moving in an oval pattern that took them beyond my range of vision.

Like trout cruising tributary mouths prior to their spawning runs, so too will trout cruise the area immediately in front of their section of shoreline. But what most anglers see is a

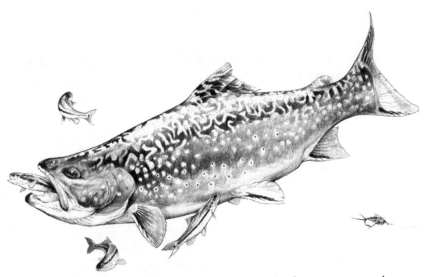

school of trout dimpling the surface, going down, reappearing farther down the shoreline and, seemingly constantly moving away.

The oval patterns that the trout create can sometimes evolve into circles or crescents, and the direction the fish are moving can reverse itself at any time. The school can also disappear and not reappear for a few hours or even until the following day. What triggers these reversals and disappearances is a continual source of bafflement to me. At times I think the wind is responsible, or large, predatory fish, or barometric pressure, or that the trout have paired off and are actually spawning.

When I am fishing, though, I concern myself with the line of travel, the length of the line the fish move along, and the width of the oval. Generally, the longer the line of travel, the wider the oval will be. For instance: The schooling trout I saw on that first day had a line of travel of approximately 100 yards, which is long for my lake. As I later discovered, however, that line matched the length of the sandbar the trout were cruising over, and the oval was probably about 50 feet across. This line of travel does not indicate the actual length of the spawning area. Indeed, where the trout eventually build their redds can be only a few feet wide.

The patterns in the lake I fish average from 100 to 150 feet long by 20 to 25 feet wide. In other small lakes and mountain tarns where I have fished for fall trout, and where tributaries have been few or nonexistent, I have found the trout cruising in patterns of similar sizes. This does not mean that patterns cannot stretch for greater distances, of course. Each lake is different, and just because a lake is big does not mean the size of the patterns will be big.

How to find these patterns requires time, patience and luck. But unlike other times of year, finding trout in fall does not demand vast knowledge of a lake's physical characteristics.

For me, the search for schooling trout usually begins in late August, when the nights become a bit cooler and the days shorter. Fish begin to stay up and in for longer periods in the mornings and evenings. And if the autumn rains come early and swell the feeder brooks, trout will run them or stay around their mouths until either the water recedes or the fish spawn. (The amount of rainfall and ambient temperatures are two key factors that anglers should always pay close attention to.)

Every day, once in early morning and again in late afternoon, I drop by the lake and, using field glasses, scan the lake's surface for a few hundred yards in all directions. If by mid-September I have not seen any schools, I take out a boat and cover the lake thoroughly. Like a hunter, I stay alert to any sound or movement; and, like an angler who stalks tarpon, bonefish and permit over saltwater flats, I am always on the lookout for moving shadows and dark masses. This can be hard work on cloudy and windy days, with each ripple seemingly possessing a dorsal fin and tail. Under such conditions I usually anchor and scan from a still position.

When I locate a school, I don't start casting immediately. Instead, I try to determine the direction in which the school is moving. I wait until I know the length of the line of travel, which I determine when they go into their vanishing act, and the width of the oval. Then I keep an eye on an imaginary line that runs from where I last saw them back to me. I can usually pick them up without any difficulty, however, for the sun is often out and their shadow is evident, or else the oval is narrow enough so that their turn into the return line of travel is easily visible. Also, since most schools I encounter in fall are in 15 to 20 feet of water, I can usually pick them up even if the sun isn't shining.

Once I have established the size of the pattern, I position myself in the center. I cast a few feet in front of the school and slightly inside, toward me; and if I hook a fish, I ease it from the school. I do not strike hard and strip in as fast as I can. Rather, I give the trout line while gently working it away from the school.

Although some anglers believe fish should be worked out of a school as fast as possible because a hooked fish emits lactic acid and alarms the others, I have found that easing them is far more successful. By easing a trout out and away, I don't disturb the school—which gives me at least one more chance to cast and hook-up before the school is either out of sight or casting range. Actually, in my experiences with still-water trout, what appears to alarm a school more than anything else is the visual impact of seeing one of their own kind fighting and twisting for survival. When a trout is bulled away from the others, the school scatters and goes down. And although it will regroup and return to the pattern, the risk of the school staying down for a long period is high.

For flies, I use streamers, wets, nymphs and dries, with No. 16 to 20 wets getting the nod 95 percent of the time. And because aquatic insect life is generally scant in my northern lake during late summer and fall, the patterns I prefer to use are terrestrials such as ants and Woolly Worms. When these two favorites do not produce, I start experimenting.

What the fall angler must keep in mind is that once he

has found the school, he then must attract the trout as well as offer up his best imitation. And although a terrestrial will usually serve both these purposes, a streamer fished near the surface or a nymph fished on top will sometimes take fish when all else fails. When trout are cruising out in front of their lairs to-be during this prespawning period, they can be very unpredictable in terms of what they will strike at. It is just then when anglers should take heed of the sage's words, "Leave no stone unturned."

Another factor that still-water anglers must contend with is the presentation of an imitation. Without a good presentation, no imitation is likely to catch trout. And during fall, when the fish are often close to the surface, the best presentations are executed on lines no heavier than Weight 5, leaders measuring nine to 20 feet, and fine tippets not thicker than 5X.

Light, floating lines are favored at this time because they will not splash heavily on the surface and send out alarming vibrations. It's also much easier to lift a light line off the water when long casts have to be made with a minimum of false casting. Leaders should be long enough to allow the fly to sink just under the surface, and to create little surface disturbance.

The exceptions to these fiats of still-water angling are when the fish are down and the wind is up. Then the angler must use heavier lines; weight-forward, rocket tapers, full-sinking, sinking-tip and so on. Leaders should be shorter so they will turn over in a stiff wind, with tippets thicker to accommodate larger flies.

For anglers who want to fish still waters for autumn brook trout but are hesitant because they do not know the water, following are a few basic tips.

For starters, maps should be procured if at all possible. Area lake-protection societies and state fish and game departments are the best sources, though it can't hurt to stop at a local tackleshop either. Most maps will delineate a lake's bottom and show where tributaries, if any, exist. If maps are not available, grab a pair of field glasses and travel around the lake either by land or boat. If the lake is a large one, then scout as much of the shoreline as is reasonably possible. Look for rising trout, of course, and for tributaries of any size. Remember to be cognizant of rainfall and ambient temperatures, for although trout will not spawn until the photoperiod is right, cold and wet weather can bring them up.

Learn to interpret shoreline characteristics. A steep, rocky shoreline will usually lead to a similar bottom. Where the shoreline slopes gently and is sandy or muddy, the lake bottom will generally follow suit. Such areas as these are excellent places to look for prespawning brook trout. But remember to first look out from the shoreline, and not close in. Where the water is shallow, head out or scan the surface where the bottom begins to drop off; the water will be cooler there and more appealing to trout.

On larger lakes, look for buoys or markers to help find potential spawning and prespawning areas. Most states place these markers around sandbars and hidden reefs as warnings for boaters. And while they mean caution to them, they mean nothing but good news to the angler.

When the leaves begin to turn to their autumn hues, and the air becomes crisp and alive with the richness of wood smoke, head for the lakes and ponds that were abandoned in mid-June. Chances are nobody else will be there. Just angler and trout and autumn. And when a school is found, a bit of the mystery of still-water fishing becomes less so. Then the angler learns something more . . . that he can never know enough, and that that is the way it should be. §

# Rainbow Trout

## A. J. McClane

*Haya! Haya! Come up again Swimmer . . . Welcome Super-*
*natural One, you Long-Life-Maker for you come to set me right*
*again as is always done by you.*

—From the Kwakiutl Indian prayers to salmon and steelhead.

T HEY COME FROM THE SEA with the first fall rains;
they come with the snows and they come when the earth
smells green. Over the bars and past winkled half-tide rocks
where sea perch and rust-colored dabs drift across their secret
paths in the kelp, they come in creeping, hesitant runs, then
halting as though drugged by an osmotic change from years in
distant deeps to that now-thin liquid forming an unlit street.
There are wraiths to be avoided—a seal, an otter or simply the
shadows of gulls. And in the precise rhythm born with time,
as the tide swells in their favor, the silver phalanx runs boldly
forward again to begin a journey that may last hundreds of
miles, where the hen will violently tail her natal stones to hide

golden pearls of spawn before she is spent and dark with winter's chill. Another color emerges too. The bright armor forged in the Pacific long gave way to a growing lateral band—the red badge of courage that is the rainbow trout. The male steelhead is newly toothed in grotesque jaws, a fierce visage, a primitive war mask for the strength he no longer enjoys. But then the rainbow is a fish of many faces, and while we may forever debate the proposition, it has only one peer as a freshwater gamefish—the Atlantic salmon.

I caught my first steelhead within a short cast of Roderick L. Haig-Brown's home on the Campbell River in British Columbia—which is like a sinner in sackcloth taking his vows with the Dalai Lama. My eastern boyhood experience with wild rainbow trout was limited, as there were few streams with reproducing populations in the Catskills: Callicoon Creek and the Esopus held river-born fish, and I occasionally caught a few big ones from the Delaware, which in those days was primarily a smallmouth bass stream. The only large migratory rainbows were in the Finger Lakes region, where my career reached its nadir on a trip to Catherine Creek. Anglers stood shoulder-to-shoulder like Gary Cooper's beady-eyed Bengal Lancers facing the Dervishes. One spawner was often hooked by two or three rods simultaneously, using frozen lumps of petroleum jelly colored with Mercurochrome, hanks of red yarn, red golf tees and other baits too bizzare to list. Except for heated debates about who caught the fish, it was as exciting as extracting sardines from a can.

A lot of gravel has rolled under foot since then. I remember that glorious summer-run ten-pounder I took on a dry fly while fishing with Pop Morris at the old Blue Creek Camp on the Klamath in California. Pop was an over-70-year-old Ichabod Crane who danced on algal slick boulders with impunity. He tied all his flies upside down, convinced that steelhead hooked in the roof of the mouth were inspired to greater heights. And there was Johnny Walatka's original tent camp on the Brooks River in Alaska, where I took Patti on our honeymoon in 1952, to catch her first 30-inch rainbow—which she carefully released. I can still see the tundra and wolf willows, the ptarmigan bursting from peavines, and still hear the methodical slap of ice-coated flyline against water in the silent world of snow. For two chilling weeks we shared one sleeping bag and a meager supply of sour mash; the urban carnality of Niagara Falls wouldn't offer much more than walleye fishing, however, which only proves the backwardness of travel agents. Although I never pursued rainbow trout with the dedication that millionaire *New York Herald* publisher James Gordon Bennet invested in his search for the perfect mutton chop (in less violent moments he was known to throw an offending chop onto the floor, and in a display of passion he bought Ciro's of Monte Carlo, a restaurant that served properly aged double-rib Southdowns, so he could dine without risk whenever he was in town). I did know that somewhere there was often one river, or one lake, that produced exceptional rainbows—not always bigger, but somehow the best of the breed.

In his scholarly work, *Steelhead Fly Fishing and Flies,* which is literally drenched with data and lore, and together with his earlier volume *Steelhead Trout* comprises more than you need to know about the anadromous rainbow, author Trey Combs observes that Dean River steelhead are the strongest of all, rivaled only by the fish of the Thompson River. This long-held angling belief was confirmed by British Columbia fishery biologists, who placed various races of steelhead in tanks and subjected the trout to currents of sustained velocities—running them on an aquatic treadmill, so to speak. The Dean and Thompson River trout proved to have as much as four times the stamina of steelhead from other watersheds. Although I haven't fished either stream since the 1950s (we went safari style to the lower Dean in a Ford tri-motor on floats), my recollection is that both produced real "tackle busters" as compared to many rivers where the trout perform nobly but without the speed and acrobatics of the Dean and Thompson strains. In common with other salmonids, particularly the Atlantic salmon, various racial stocks of rainbow differ in their fighting ability. Any opinion as to which is the better gamefish must take into account a number of factors, and size is usually the first thing that comes to mind.

One might expect that the bigger the fish the greater its resistance, but in my experience that just isn't true. The rainbow I will never forget was a 16¾-pounder I took from Michigan's Au Sable River in October 1971 while fishing with Paul Harvey. I have taken heavier fish elsewhere, but never one that was almost continuously airborne—leaping, cartwheeling, doing bellywhoppers like a kid on a Flexible Flyer. In what may seem like hyperbole, it actually churned across the surface in the posture of a greyhounding marlin. This deep-bodied 32-inch trout, a record for the Au Sable, was canonized by a local taxidermist and now hangs on its walnut plaque in the Lakewood Shores bar at Oscoda—in tribute to its demise. I sank over my wader tops and finally sat in a frigid backwater while slowly steering that fish into my lap. After 25 minutes of acrobatics, it was as dead as the proverbial doornail. Not even in the salad days of Peru's Lake Titicaca, when 16- to 18-pound fish were par for the course and the daily scorecard might include a 27-, 28- or even a 30-pounder (with the lake record at 34 pounds), did any of these fish provide more than a competent performance—one, maybe two jumps, then a sullen tug-of-war, *thump, thump, thump,* like a gut-busting grouper trying to find a hole in the coral. It didn't matter whether the trout were caught in the lake or its tributary streams. But on a still morning at 14,000 feet, when a giant rainbow rolls out of crystalline water and shatters the mirrored surface into a hundred images of itself, well, the overture was better than the opera and that's often what angling is all about.

One of the "hottest" inland rainbow fisheries today is the

Bow River in Alberta. The strain of trout found there seldom grows into double-digit figures, but these fish have more bounce to the ounce. The four- and five-pounders wheel into the current and get into your backing like bonefish, and everybody who visits the stream is impressed by their stamina. As much as I delight in catching rainbows in the Yellowstone and Madison, those fish just aren't in the same league.

When we speak of a strain or race of trout, it may encompass a subspecies; and while the latter term is useful to designate salmonids of a particular watershed, it has little meaning in making taxonomic distinctions. Many rainbow populations have been isolated for untold thousands of years, and some morphological separation inevitably occurred. When Jordan and Evermann were cataloging our trout in 1902 (*American Food and Game Fishes*), it was believed that a number of rainbow subspecies, even distinct species, existed. The major differences described other than coloration and spotting were in the scale counts. Some 30 years later, however, Dr. Charles M. Mottley discovered that these meristics in the rainbow were a reflection of existing environmental conditions during early de-

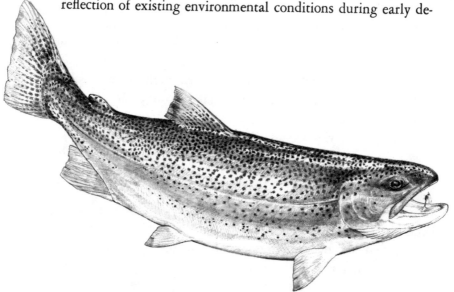

velopment of the fish. For example, the progeny of rainbows from Kootenay Lake, British Columbia, showed scale counts that varied according to the time of egg deposition. The difference was related to water temperature. Fish resulting from a spawn that occurred late in the run and at a higher temperature varied from the population as a whole, with the number of scale rows decreasing. An even greater change was induced by rearing fish at a higher temperature in a hatchery, with the number of scale rows decreasing further as the temperature increased.

Today, sophisticated phylogenetic studies are based on the amino acid sequence of protein molecules and the relationship between the chromosomes of different genotypes. As with the brook trout, a century of domestication—especially in the midwestern and eastern United States—had a tremendous impact on the rainbow, diluting the "genetic message" in some cases and delivering a new version in others. The domestic Whitney strain, for example, was derived from McCloud River stock at the turn of the century and was apparently crossed at various times with steelhead from the Eel River and Lahontan cutthroat from Lake Tahoe—a rather sporty heritage. Drawing a composite picture of the rainbow is almost impossible, however. The Kamloops rainbow subspecies spawns in the spring, the domestic Wisconsin strain spawns in the fall, the domestic Shasta strain spawns in the winter, and while seven years is usually given as a maximum lifespan, some of the unsullied Alaskan strains live to 12 years or more. There has also been a continuous recruitment of different domestic stocks in many river systems over a long period, plus natural hybridization with the golden and cutthroat trout in water throughout western United States.

Native only to western North America, *Salmo gardineri* was long ago given a passport to all the clear-flowing waters of the world, places as far removed as the Urubamba, the Sacred

River of the Incas that rises at an altitude among the clouds and then plunges past the ruins of Machu Picchu before raging down the eastern slopes of the Andes into the Amazon. If you have lungs like bellows and can run behind a hooked trout along almost perpendicular rapids, fishing that river is a fascinating experience. The Urubamba makes Oregon's turbulent McKenzie River look like a leaky faucet. There are also unnamed lakes in the ridges that still hold 20-pound trout.

While the presence of rainbows in New Zealand is by now legendary, their southernmost latitude is in the Kerguelen Islands opposite Antarctica (which is hard to find unless you turn the globe upside down). One of the most successful introductions in recent history occurred at Lake Nahuel Haupi in Argentina. Originally planted with rainbow trout in 1901, the lake produced fabulous brown trout but only *ho hum* rainbow fishing; in fact, the rainbows led a monklike existence at benthic depths and were caught only in modest sizes by deep trolling. Then, in 1965, Argentina imported rainbow eggs from Denmark, which is about as logical as Tokyo importing cars from Detroit. Of course, Denmark originally secured its rainbows from the United States and made trout farming into one of its leading export food industries. This highly pampered stock, which I sampled in the meadow streams of Jutland one summer with artist Svend Saabye, was reminiscent of the precision-tooled drones New York's Cortland hatchery turned out in the 1930s—seemingly bred for quick delivery to the skillet, they displayed all the fighting instincts of Roberto Duran in his infamous eighth round with Sugar Ray Leonard. But the rainbows that were hatched at the federal fish station in Bariloche apparently had Peter Benchley's great white shark in their bloodline. According to Dr. Miguel de Lourdes Baiz, one macho male brood fish bit a tourist on the forefinger as he innocently pointed at the trout in a holding pool.

The day I visited de Lourdes Baiz, he was busy installing

screens over the pools because some of the trout kept jumping onto the bank in blind panic everytime anybody walked by. This was the same problem that Seth Green mentioned of his Caledonia hatchery in 1874—generations of domestication had yet to breed out that wild reaction to escape. After the fish from Hamlet's Mad Kingdom were stocked, the change that occurred in Lake Nahuel Haupi's fishing by 1971 was so radical that local anglers actually believed a new species of trout had evolved. These silvery, deep-bodied, emerald-backed fish with heads like arrows went on a constant rampage chasing baitfish in *shallow* water. Rainbows up to 26 pounds were taken by flyfishermen casting from shore. They reminded me of the wild Kamloops trout of British Columbia, but their spiritual resemblance to a bright steelhead won the name-game, so its Spanish synonym "plateado" now separates those rainbows found in the littoral zone from the benthic population. It's possible that the plateado originated in one of Denmark's saltwater hatcheries, and untangling its genesis would make an index for *Gulliver's Travels.*

But there is another element in trout fishing that cannot be measured with a tape or scale. I remember our numerous trips to the very top of the Gros Ventre River in Wyoming. There was, and perhaps still is, a population of small rainbows in that river, each with lavender parr marks in perfect heart shapes. They resembled the work of a Hallmark designer. Patti called them her Valentine trout. I don't believe we ever caught a fish bigger than ten inches, but the sheer beauty of the place— with wild flowers surrounding meadow pools, and moose and elk roaming nearby—is beyond my capacity for wielding language. And the first thing that comes to mind about Chile, a country that is laced with rainbow trout streams, is not the fishing which I knew at its best, but the crisp roasted lamb the *boateros* cooked over an open fire, the good red wines and great ripe peaches. Two years ago Keith Gardner and I fished the Morice River in British Columbia, and while I recall catching some nice steelhead, it was the sapphire-blue pools, tall timber and granite ledges cloaked in morning fog above Mile Post 32 that made the trip special. It's a wild stream that leaps and roars in its den and, sadly, will soon be tamed by civilization.

Then there is the learning experience through other, perhaps wiser eyes. I once made a movie on steelhead fishing for the National Film Board of Canada. During the three-week-long shooting, I enjoyed the company of a Kwakiutl Indian guide named Phil. At our lunch break one day, we were sitting on a high bank when a group of steelhead, maybe a dozen in all, tried to ford the shallow bar at the stream mouth during a rapidly falling tide. The fish milled around with their backs out of water, dashed halfway across the bar, found virtually no water, and then turned back again. It was strange behavior for any predator-conscious migrant in bright daylight. Finally the fish plunged ahead and, wiggling violently on wet bellies, churned those last few yards into the deeper riffle above. I asked Phil why the steelhead didn't wait for a rising tide? His answer, though allegorical, could not be faulted. He looked at me as though I was asking Albert Einstein to correct a high school algebra paper.

"The swimmers, who are led by their chief, come from remote villages under the sea. They send their scouts ahead, and if the scouts do not safely pass, the other swimmers will not come. It has always been so."

I didn't ask Phil how the scouts sent the good word back to the villages. It somehow reminded me of that classic explanation that Louis Armstrong used when asked about the meaning of jazz: "If you got to ask, baby, you ain't never gonna' know." §

# Two

*Jack McLaughlin*

GOLDEN NOVEMBER DAYS kindle the spirit and the yearning to be afield with finely muscled bird dogs amid golden sedge or aspen. The location matters little. It is you and your hunting pal, the guy with whom you have shared those memorable days with grand dogs pointing proudly, and the thrill of a proper double highlighted by stirring retrieves. In all of the world there is no doubt that the relationship between two bird hunters is the strongest kind. To paraphrase with due respect for the late Mr. Havilah Babcock: "Bird hunting, like marriage, was certainly made for two."

You have experienced the camaraderie of a deer camp, and shared a duck blind with a couple of fine friends. You have trout fished from Montana to Missouri with some of the world's finest, but the fondest memories that you shall ever cherish are those spent afield with your bird hunting pal. The other guy may be a doctor or a farmer or a mechanic. He may have been educated at Harvard or a seventh-grade dropout at P.S. 103.

The relationship is inseparable and you keep in touch throughout the year. There is that litter of puppies by your top gun dog to pick and cull and the endless conversation about blood lines, nose, style, and conformation. Is a big dog better than a little dog? Are setters better than pointers? How is the bird crop and when will you next make another trip to your favorite covers to check things out? Where will your annual jaunts take you this year? What about Montana for sharptails or Michigan for ruffed grouse? Or perhaps a quail hunt in Kansas is in order. You heard the birds are coming back again in Kansas.

You spend weekends training young dogs or hunting for a bargain in old doubles. Should you buy a vintage Fox or Parker or try an A.Y.A. or a Bernadelli? What chokes are best? These guns shoot such tight patterns today because of the collars used in modern shotshells. Perhaps you can devise some spreader loads of your own to open up the old bird gun for shooting in heavy brush. Many a winter afternoon after season's end is spent hand-loading shells and patterning guns to determine maximum efficiency. After all, it pays to know what your favorite bird gun will do when you are in the field. There are the equipment catalogs to peruse. You will need some new dog collars and stake-out chains. Be sure to order the stake-out chains in time. Bird season will be coming on in another ten months.

How about trading some outdoor books to read? I'll let you have my Nash Buckingham if you let me see those books that you have by Ray Holland and Havilah Babcock. Throw in some Christmas issues of the *"Field."* I sure get tired of the "how-to-do-it" stories that the outdoor mags are running these days. What ever happened to the "Me and Joe" stories of years gone by? I can recall getting plenty of instruction from those old time writers woven into a piece about a favorite gunning expedition. Ray Holland was an expert at it.

Winter gives way to Spring and the solitude of turkey hunting. You start to think about working those January pups. There is the endless yard training and the teaching of "Whoa," "Heel," and "Come here." You have "worked" them in the field letting them chase larks, but the time has come to teach them manners and how to handle real birds. You need to build a recall pen for quail. There is that training field that you must see the farmer about using. You can't rush those pups but they will need some learning before summer's doldrums are upon you. Young Dan is coming along, you both agree. Little Sue still chases butterflies but you think she will make it big some day. The old dogs—Mack and Jed and Jimmy—are looking good; you hope you can keep them on the right track. Maybe they could use some more yard training.

Summer arrives and it is too hot to work dogs. It's time to go fishing. Shall we take a float in the Ozarks or go to Montana for some fine dry fly fishing for browns and rainbows? Better get your wives and kids together for a barbecue to talk things over. I'll bring the trap and some shells and we'll let the family shoot some clay targets. I guess we had better take Jane and Mary out to dinner pretty soon or they will think that we have gone to the dogs completely. Maybe they'd like to go on a camping and fishing trip. Summer is fun but it seems to last six months. When can we go bird hunting again?

Time to reminisce. Remember the time you flushed the quail down the toilet in the motel in Kansas? You told the owner you weren't cleaning birds in the room, just letting the water drain out before you put them on ice. He gave you that incredible look that usually means "Don't come back." You know because you have seen it a time or two before during the last thirty years.

There was the time at the old railroad hotel when you put the birds on the windowsill to chill them, and the cat carried them off during the night. That's the time we used the stop sign in the street to shore up the canvas we had covering the dog crates during the ice storm. We sure felt sheepish when we went to unveil the street sign as the local police looked on.

Do you recall the time the dogs started barking at three in the morning and the traveling salesman came beating at the door in his long underwear? He was really mad but after all *it was* about three degrees above zero. After raising hell with the dogs for barking we found a live quail parading about among the dog crates. It had escaped from my hunting jacket. Poor dogs, no wonder they got excited!

I'm sure glad you stopped smoking. There was the time you were running that young Jim dog and he made his first point. He retrieved the bird to hand when you shot it for him and you discovered your pants were on fire because you were so excited that you put the cigar in your pocket.

I never will forget the time Jed pointed the covey that ran into the groundhog hole. They came out one at a time as he stood like a statue, then routed them when he saw that we didn't believe his find. We missed every one of them without touching a feather. Well, nobody really believes that one anyway.

You know, I still chuckle about the time that we fixed the television set in the motel room because it was fuzzy. It really wasn't very funny when the owner came to the door of our smoke-filled room after you crossed the wires inadvertently. Even though we did pay him to get the set repaired, I don't think we are exactly welcome anymore. You will recall he is the same fellow who said he didn't mind us cooking in the room, until the time I fell asleep and burned the chili and black soot poured out of the door you left cracked for ventilation. You know, our places to stay are getting fewer all the time.

THERE WAS THE TIME we got stopped by the highway patrol for not having any tail lights. That was really hard to explain until we discovered that one of the pups had gotten out of his crate and chewed the wires in half. That was the same night you dropped the car keys in the weeds when the birds flushed right near the front bumper. I thought we'd never find those keys in the dark. You never did believe in carrying extras until that event.

The two guys who challenged us to a bird hunting contest got a surprise when they took us to "new territory." You and I came to find we had been hunting the place for years but didn't let on about it. They really were mad when they found us back at the car drinking a beer with the limit in our coats when they only had six birds between them. It cost them only five bucks apiece and I don't know why it made them so mad. Ozark folk are sometimes kind of peculiar.

How about old Jim, the dog we bought from the field trial fellow? He could find birds, but I never thought we'd ever get him broke. That was a good idea of yours to hide in the weeds at the place the covey used. I remember I let you off to hide out and took Jim up the road and turned him loose. He busted two coveys before he got to where you were waiting as he chased a bird about to light. He was the most surprised dog in the world when you stepped out of your hide and said "Whoa," then commenced to entreat him to do better while you applied a goodly application of hickory switch. I don't think I recall Jim ever breaking birds after that, do you?

That time we got stuck on the ridge coming out of the big bottom is one I can't forget. The ground thawed by the time we got back to the truck that night. We could see flame coming out of the barrels at last light as I recall. Then we were just plumb stuck in the mud and the truck wouldn't start. I thought we would freeze for sure sleeping in the barn with nothing but hay for a cover. But we made it out with a tractor from the old man the next morning. The dogs helped to keep us warm, rooting right into the hay with us. I can still hear those birds calling as the sun went down. I remember the starshine and moonglow through that hole in the barn roof where the big oak blew down and came through. It's funny some of the things you remember, isn't it?

Those dogs can cause you some trouble, too. Sometimes I think we should have gone to vet school. Remember when Jim had the heart attack in the field and we had to give him cardiac massage? You learned about that from your son, Dick, after he graduated from veterinarian studies. Then there was old Ben who had the seizures, and we figured it out to be low blood sugar and fed him Hershey bars. I remember that time out in Kansas when I gave him two Hersheys instead of one. We argued about that and you were right. I can see Ben to this day fading from view on that Kansas prairie like a field trial all-age dog running in a stake somewhere up in Canada. If he wasn't such a good gun dog I would have considered running him in some trials, but I never gave him more than one chocolate bar after that episode.

I thought we never would get old Jack over killing chickens. I'll never forget the time that we had him on a leash and went to ask that farmer if he'd permit us to hunt. He came out of the back door to meet us as we stood at the gate to his yard. When he opened the gate three chickens shot past him and into the path of old Jack, and he killed all three before you could jerk him up. I can still see old Jack on his last hunt, nearly blind and running into an occasional tree. Right before we picked him up for the last time, he pointed a bird that you shot which then landed in the fork of a small tree.

Do you remember the time that some prankster let the air out of our tires and we had to walk five miles to town? I didn't think that was too funny, especially after we got back and found one of the pups had gotten out of his crate and had eaten five birds. It didn't seem to upset his stomach or his appetite, though.

You and I got along all these years pretty well. Oh, we have had our ups and downs and we don't always agree on everything. I had an invitation to go hunting at that fancy plantation and you said you weren't interested in hunting with all that formality. It sure made me mad. You said we would have to wear a suit and tie to dinner, and fancy hunting clothes, and act our best for all of those "genteel folk." Where'd you ever learn big words like "genteel"? Now as I remember it, you said we wouldn't be able to cook in the room and no carousing in honky tonks. There would be cocktails before dinner, and dress up parties, and everyone acting their best, and who wants that? You said you liked roughing it better and, you know, after all these years, so do I.

There was the time on the way home that you and I got into a more than serious discussion about politics and you said we should stop the car, get out, and cool off. When you stepped out of the car you fell nearly out of sight into a deep snow drift, and I took off down the road like I was going to leave you. When I came back a little later you sure were cooled off. I think it took you an hour to get warmed up.

We have had lots of laughter and some serious moments too, like the time you had your first little warning of a heart problem on a quail hunt with me. I thought there was something wrong but you said nothing about it, and I guess even Mary didn't know for a while after I was aware of it.

YES, A COUPLE OF GUYS can get pretty close in thirty years of bird hunting and traveling around with dogs. A lot of things happen that wouldn't otherwise, and most of them are good. We have come a long way since I got back from Korea. You had to give up a good business and I got a couple of teeth knocked out playing hockey because I didn't have enough sense to know when to quit. Some fine old pointers and setters have gone to the big place over yonder where all good dogs go. We have seen lots of good dogs work, you and I, and we've managed some good shooting now and then. Remember the time you forgot to change barrels and still you managed to kill two birds with your first shot and another with your second shot from a full-choked gun?

You get closer to a person bird hunting. It's all part of pointing dogs, whirring wings, and popping guns, especially when there is just us two. §

# Acknowledgments

James Dean Quail *by Thomas McIntyre (page 49) reprinted from* Sports Afield—*September 1982. Copyright © The Hearst Corporation. All rights reserved.*

Downstream *by Jim Capossela (page 54) reprinted from* Sports Afield—*February 1982. Copyright © The Hearst Corporation. All rights reserved.*

The Pheasant *by William Childress (page 62) reprinted from* Sports Afield—*February 1981. Copyright © The Hearst Corporation. All rights reserved.*

Pardonable Sins *by Lionel Atwill (page 67) reprinted from* Sports Afield—*February 1982. Copyright © The Hearst Corporation. All rights reserved.*

The Everyday Letort *by Harrison O'Connor (page 125) reprinted from* Sports Afield—*March 1981. Copyright © The Hearst Corporation. All rights reserved.*

Old Friend Now Departed *by Pete Kaminsky (page 137) reprinted from* Sports Afield—*January 1982. Copyright © The Hearst Corporation. All rights reserved.*

Shorebird Hunting: The Way It Was *by Paul Rundell (page 143) reprinted from* Sports Afield—*May 1981. Copyright © The Hearst Corporation. All rights reserved.*

Roll-Your-Own Fishing *by Vance Bourjaily (page 162) reprinted from* Sports Afield—*February 1982. Copyright © The Hearst Corporation. All rights reserved.*

Still-Water Trout *by David Seybold (page 183) reprinted from* Sports Afield—*October 1982. Copyright © The Hearst Corporation. All rights reserved.*